RUNAWAYS

AWESOMENESS INK

LOS ANGELES • NEW YORK

Created and produced by Running Press Kids,
an imprint of Running Press Book Publishers, Philadelphia, PA 19103.

Printed in the United States of America

ISBN 978-1-941341-08-7
Library of Congress Control Number: 2014941577

10 9 8 7 6 5 4 3 2 1
Digit on the right indicates the number of this printing
09182014-C-2

Cover image: rappensuncle / istock.com

Visit awesomenessink.com

AWESOMENESS TV

R U N A W A Y S

A novel by
BETH SZYMKOWSKI

based on the series created by
BETH SZYMKOWSKI

Olivia Abernathy stood staring down at the closed trunk of her husband's white Mercedes. Dark streaks of blood marred the otherwise pristine surface.

It was not what she'd expected to find when she woke that morning and found his side of the bed empty. Again.

She'd risen with the grace of the dancer she once was, a ballerina with plans to tour the world on her toes until she fell for William Abernathy IV. He was a gorgeous playboy from a wealthy family, accustomed to money solving all the problems his fast living created. When he smiled, her dreams and every- thing else fell away.

She'd dressed and made her way to the kitchen, where she poured a finger of orange juice into the cut-glass tumbler, then added vodka to the rim before gulping it down. Breakfast of champions. The sting in her throat was familiar and soothing. It wouldn't be long before her body would warm and relax from its effects.

She grabbed her keys and made for the garage. Inside, she was surprised to see William's car in his parking spot next to hers. If he didn't sleep in their bed and hadn't gone anywhere in his car, where was he? She'd moved to look inside the frosted windows when . . . *WHAM!* Her feet flew out from under her. Her head bounced on the concrete floor. She floundered, trying to right herself, but the floor was slick with something and the more she moved, the more she slipped. Finally, she pulled herself up, taking care like she would if she were standing on ice. She inhaled deeply, regaining her composure, and stared down at her white shift dress.

It was covered in bright red blood.

Olivia fought the scream that was rising fast like bile in her throat. She clenched her mouth shut and told herself to hold it together. She was not a screamer. She was calm in a crisis. It was one of her better qualities. Her ability to remain unruffled in difficult situations was the reason the Danbury Country Club's social chair was always calling her when things were falling apart.

But a sizable pool of blood on the garage floor was definitely different than trouble with an overwhelmed caterer or temperamental florist. Olivia focused on her breathing and stared at the dark puddle. It was large and extended to underneath the back of William's car. Someone had dragged something or someone to his trunk.

What the hell had happened? William had made his share of enemies in the business world and had a remarkably relative sense of personal ethics, but he'd never been involved in anything violent. Violence was ugly and he was anything but.

When a car drove by outside, Olivia moved into action. She couldn't allow the occupants to see her soiled dress or the slick, red floor. She quickly closed the garage door, realizing what she did next would be dictated by what she found inside the trunk. She braced herself, staring at the closed lid.

Ordinarily, it would be empty, save for the built-in jack and spare tire and maybe William's golf clubs. He was very fastidious that way. He liked things to feel unused and got a new car every two years, as soon as the new-car smell wore off. Olivia was the opposite. While she obviously always drove a luxury vehicle, and wouldn't drive anything more than five years old, she detested having to learn all the bells and whistles of a new ride. She wanted to know how to turn on the windshield wipers without thinking about it. It was typical of their differences. William had always been looking for things to entertain him, much like a child wanting an endless supply of new toys. Luckily, he had a generous trust fund to support his needs. He also worked and appeared to be successful, but Olivia knew his earnings could never support his lifestyle.

She couldn't put it off much longer. She needed to open the damn thing and see what, or who, was inside.

Her hand shook as she pressed the button on the car remote. She braced herself as the trunk slowly opened. Given the size of the bloodstain on the garage floor, she felt certain whoever, or whatever, was in the trunk would be a particularly gruesome sight. She let out a slow exhalation when she saw no signs of the mayhem that had to have occurred, but only the shape of a body wrapped in blankets and sheets.

She took a broom from where it leaned nearby and poked the pile with the handle, not sure what would happen. She half expected somebody to pop up and yell, "Boo!" The thought oddly amused her.

She poked again. Nothing. She tried again, this time firmly pressing the wood into the mound. A red spot appeared, flowering as the wetness spread into a large crimson stain.

Taking another breath, Olivia pulled back the covers to see whom William had killed.

1. MASON AND KAYLEE ARE MISSING

Trevor Anthony sat with a handful of students in the sun-dappled hallway outside the Danbury Prep administrative offices, waiting to be questioned by the police. The grave faces of past Danbury leaders stared down at them from photos lining the wall.

The students gathered were an unusual mix, from one of the oddest girls in school to the class president. Trevor thought of himself as the class eunuch. He was popular with the girls because of his polished style and sharp wit, but, of course, he never had a relationship with any of them. Their parts didn't match the way he wanted them to.

Keesha Washington spoke first. That was typical. Keesha was usually the first one to raise her hand in class. Always straight up, like she was raising a signal flag. "Kaylee didn't come to first period," she said. Keesha and Kaylee had been best friends since the beginning of freshman year three years ago. She was a bit hurt that Kaylee clearly was involved in something major and she knew nothing about it, but Keesha wasn't about to show her feelings to anyone else. She always behaved in a professional manner. Her long auburn hair was tucked behind her ears, revealing dainty pearl earrings.

"Mason wasn't there either," added Glinda Adams. Glinda, on the other hand, was all about flash. Everything about her called attention to herself. She wore an assortment of seven-inch platform shoes and had long blonde hair tinted green near the ends: the perfect complement to her prep-school plaid skirt and blazer, of course.

Mason Henry and Kaylee Abernathy were the most controversial couple at the school. She was a well-liked cheerleader and he was a charity case with a perpetual chip on his shoulder. People either delighted in the inherent romance of such a mismatch or took bets on how long before it flamed out. Glinda gave them three months max. But even she had no idea it would end with authorities involved.

"I don't see why we had to get called out of class to answer questions about them cutting." Keesha shook her head. "If I miss my Orgo test and all she did was ditch, Kaylee will be so sorry."

"Please. Tell me you don't think we're all being interrogated because two people cut class?" Lily Mars was annoyed. "I thought this school was supposed to cater to society's elite, not society's imbecilic."

"Is that even a word?" asked Keesha. "My point is that something bigger is going on," Lily glared at her.

"She's right," said Glinda. "Cutting is not a crime for the cops."

"Does anybody care what you think?" Lily shot Glinda a withering look. She didn't care if she was agreeing with her; at no point was the little toad to think they were on friendly terms together. Lily was the de facto social leader of the school. Glinda was a loser. The fact that they were sitting anywhere near each other and were engaged in the same discussion was remarkable. Glinda was well aware of the social divides and that she was crossing them. She smiled sweetly at Lily and batted her eyes.

"People are saying they ran away." Keesha crossed her ankles and folded her hands in her lap. Rumors were flying fast through everyone's phones. One chain of texts had Mason withdrawing a large sum of money at an ATM near the Canadian border and another had them both spotted at the airport waiting to board a flight to Belize. Keesha knew that was wrong. Kaylee had been to Belize and hated the humidity.

"I heard Kaylee's room was messed up," Trevor said to no one in particular. He was worried. Kaylee had been extremely upset last night, and he hoped she hadn't done anything irrational.

"So's mine," Glinda mused.

"Why doesn't that surprise me?" Lily shook her head. What the hell was she doing here?

"Kaylee's usually neat. Weirdly neat." Trevor considered that a compliment. Kaylee was one of the few people Trevor would ever consider living with because they shared an aversion to clutter.

Senior class president Jared Slater spoke for the first time. He'd been pacing, unable to hold his long and muscular body still. "Who cares how clean her room was? How can that be relevant?"

"Because if it's been ransacked, that means something happened," Keesha explained.

"Or if it's just slightly messy, maybe she packed in a hurry and then ran away." Trevor's mind was racing.

Neither idea sat well with Jared. He had dated Kaylee briefly a few months ago but then she broke up with him. He never stopped liking her. Jared was dismayed she ended up with a thug like Mason and thought she was crying out for help in some way. When she was ready to date someone more appropriate, he planned to take her back without holding any of her bad choices against her. He refused to believe she would run away with Mason. Even cutting wasn't like Kaylee. She was one of the good girls.

"What should we tell them?" Trevor blurted out. He'd never been involved in anything like getting questioned by the police and he wasn't sure how forthcoming he should be. "What if they ran away and don't want to be found?"

Trevor knew Kaylee loved Mason—or thought she did. And though he didn't say it to the group, he was pretty sure her home life was far from ideal.

"What if Mason took her and she didn't want to go?" Jared asked.

"You're pathetic," Lily snapped. They all knew about his thing for Kaylee, but to them he was just clinging to something that would never happen. They'd tried dating and Kaylee didn't like it that much. It was so typical that Jared's take on their being missing would be that Mason was somehow the bad guy and Kaylee was just a damsel in distress.

"Are you all forgetting what happened last night? They broke up at the party. He threatened her. She would not have run away with him."

"He was definitely angry," Glinda said with a nod.

"Maybe they made up after the party." Trevor shrugged.

"Right," Jared said sarcastically. "They went from screaming at each other in public to deciding they were going to elope in the course of one night?"

"Who said anything about eloping?" Trevor shot back.

Lily was annoyed with them all. Why did people care so much about what happened to Kaylee and Mason? "Maybe this has nothing to do with running away. Maybe they're the victims of something awful. Maybe a serial killer came and hacked them both into little pieces."

That, Keesha thought, would be a good reason to pull her out of Orgo.

2.OUTSIDERS AND SECRETS

"Since when are a couple of runaways a reason to interrogate half the school?"

Lily smiled sweetly at the two police detectives sitting across from her even though her blonde head was throbbing, a reminder of how much she drank at Keesha's party the night before. She'd managed to cover the dark circles under her eyes and had expertly applied Le Métier de Beauté foundation to the delicate features of her face. She'd quickly pulled her hair back with a clip as she was running out the door that morning, but she still managed to rock it. Lily never had to work very hard to look good.

"We ask the questions," stated the older detective. Lily thought his name was O'Malley or O'Rourke or something that sounded like it belonged on an Irish bar. "We were talking about how Mason and Kaylee met."

"Why do you think I would be the person to ask about that?" Lily asked pointedly.

"Here's how this works," the man said, his irritation showing. "I ask the questions. You answer them." He paused for effect. "Now. How did Mason and Kaylee meet?"

"I don't know how they met. I'm guessing it was at school because they didn't exactly move in the same circles anywhere else."

"They were from different backgrounds?"

"Her father runs a multinational company. His father cleans toilets."

The detective nodded and wrote something in his notebook. He looked completely out of place in the clubby atmosphere of the wood-paneled teacher's lounge. Lily knew something big was going on. When students at Danbury Prep ditched, Dean Van de Sant might call their parents and apologetically question them about the whereabouts of their offspring, all while begging forgiveness for interrupting their important jobs and important lives. He wouldn't call the police. Calling in an outsider would violate a sacred rule among the elite who made up the school's population: what happens at Danbury stays at Danbury. The Danbury parents who chose to work instead of live off their trust funds became society's leaders—judges, surgeons, CEOs of Fortune 500 companies. They were the kind of people who made the rules and expected others to follow. They believed they didn't have ordinary problems, unless you counted problems with the help. On the rare occasion something needed to be dealt with, Danbury parents handled it quietly and effectively.

But here Lily was, sitting in the mahogany-paneled teacher's lounge across from two detectives wearing cheap ties. The older one looked more world-weary. He probably drank beer from a can and ate processed cheese. The other was younger and had an athletic build. He spoke well and had a decent haircut, but nothing could compensate for the polyester tie. It was like an advertisement screaming that he made less than six figures. Mason would pick a tie like that, Lily thought, if he ever actually picked a tie. At school he wore the one dictated by the uniform policy, but he would never wear a tie of his own volition.

What had he and Kaylee gotten themselves into? Had they been caught climbing the municipal water tower? Five-fingering a pack of cigarettes at the service station? Lily was sure it was something that would appeal to Kaylee's idea that she was living dangerously, without actually being dangerous. She and Mason were conspicuously absent from Homeroom that morning, an absence Lily enjoyed. She was sick of their constant mooning over each other. They were in love and wanted the world to see. How banal. Lily was in love herself, real love, not like the juvenile slobberings of those two.

"Were you at the party last night?" the detective asked.

"Of course I was at the party last night. Everyone was at the party." Lily rolled her eyes. She wasn't about to fill in the blanks for the cops. Not because she felt particularly antagonistic toward them at the moment. Truth was, she couldn't remember much of the night. She'd gotten to Keesha's after it was in full swing. Of course she would never be the first to arrive anywhere. Lily had a few G&Ts immediately. Keesha always had good gin, good liquor in general. The little uptight twit was a control freak and just would not allow for anything that might tarnish her hostessing image. When people brought a cheap handle to add to the bar, Keesha thanked them enthusiastically and then put it aside when they weren't looking. Lily had seen her own mother do that when some of her father's underlings brought subpar wine to a dinner party. That was the wine Lily stole when she needed a quick fix. Her mother didn't even bother putting it in the wine cellar and probably forgot about it the second she stuck it in a dusty corner of the pantry. She would never notice the amount of bottles back there stayed almost the same.

Lily remembered dancing. She loved to dance. It made her feel like she was flying. And she remembered, vaguely, seeing Mason alone. He'd gone into the bathroom and she'd followed him. She wasn't sure exactly why. She had her own boyfriend after all, and she was never really attracted to Mason, but he was a challenge. He should have liked Lily but he never showed any interest. He was all about Kaylee and that irked her. For whatever reason, maybe because she'd had a fair share of Tanqueray, she decided to see if she could tempt him and stir things up a bit. If something happened, it would take Kaylee down a few notches and make her own boyfriend jealous. But when Lily slipped into the bathroom after him and made it clear she was available for more than just friendship, Mason recoiled. Recoiled. Like she was repulsive. He went even further and told her he knew damaging information about her. The message was clear: back off or be sorry. Lily was furious.

"Did you talk to Kaylee last night?" The younger detective interrupted her thoughts.

"No."

"Are you two friends?"

"We move in the same social circles, but she's never been okay with my being so much more popular."

"If Kaylee and Mason were going to run off together, where would they go?" The younger detective looked up from his notebook.

Lily shook her head. "Kaylee would never run off with Mason. He was a bad boy from a nothing family."

"Right. His father cleans toilets. I remember that." The older detective nodded.

"If this Mason was so wrong for her, why would Kaylee be with him?" the younger detective continued.

"I don't know. Pick your reason: because he's uncomplicated. Or maybe she has low self-esteem and feels she can't do better than the janitor's son." The older detective nodded like this was useful information and wrote something else in his notepad. Lily sensed he might be mocking her. She wondered briefly what the detectives' parents did for a living. It was likely they would relate to Mason more than Kaylee or anyone else at the school. They were probably judging her because she had a better upbringing than they did. So typical. People didn't understand that being wealthy came with its own stresses.

"Maybe she feels dirty when she's with him and it turns her on." Lily leaned forward as she spoke. "Or the one thing everybody knows is true. He's got a pony in his pants. It's the only thing he has resembling a birthright."

She waited for their response—but nothing. They let the comment hang in the air and stared silently at her until she was forced to sit back in her chair.

"I don't know why she was with him, but I know she wouldn't run away with him. It's just not the way we do things around here. Her father would never allow it."

"You know what her father would and wouldn't allow?" The younger detective acted impressed. "What else can you tell me about Kaylee's home life?"

"Her mother is cold. Her father is charming. You'd lose her sister, Anne, if she stood against a white wall. Are we done here?"

"Please, be patient." He smiled. "You're giving us valuable information. It may not seem like it, but you are. Now help me understand how you know Kaylee's family so well."

"We all know everybody's families," Lily explained. "We've socialized together for forever."

"You know everybody's families? But not Mason's, of course."

The younger detective smiled.

"Of course not Mason's. He doesn't really count."

3. LOVERS MEET

Mason Henry sat outside Jeremy Van de Sant's office, waiting for an ass-reaming. He was all too familiar with the uncomfortable wooden seats that made his lean glutes go numb within minutes of sitting. With all the money floating around the place, Mason wondered why they couldn't pony up for cushions. Dean Van de Sant probably wanted people waiting to see him to be uncomfortable so he'd have a tactical advantage over them. What an asswipe.

Mason usually ended up in one of the seats because he routinely embarrassed his teachers by knowing more than they did about their subjects. His crime this time, however, was achieving a perfect score on his Calc test. The instructor, a man whose mustache dropped dandruff into his oolong as he drank, thought Mason had cheated. It drove the guy nuts that his least favorite student was also his best one.

Another one of the faculty's least favorites sat a few seats down from Mason. Glinda Adams was either the school freak or a rabid fashionista, depending on how you looked at her. She was weird for sure, but she was a free spirit who, like Mason, didn't seem to care about offending people. In some ways, Glinda had bigger balls than he did. Mason was raised to be independent before being plunked down in the Danbury pool of groupthink. All he did was adamantly refuse to give in to the pressure to change. He was true to his upbringing and himself no matter where he was. Glinda was raised by people who surely trained her to play nice and not make waves, but she rejected that way of living outright. She was true to herself but not her upbringing. Mason knew that took guts.

Mason didn't know it, but Glinda had no legitimate reason for sitting outside of Van de Sant's office. Whenever she cut class she usually ended up somewhere in the vicinity. She liked to see who was in trouble waiting for punishment and she liked the idea of breaking the rules right under the nose of the main disciplinarian. Glinda knew a big secret about the man and wasn't particularly afraid he'd take any action against her.

"Anger does not control me," Mason repeated to himself. "I control my anger." Screw that bullshit. He'd been forced to take a class on anger management after a fight at his old school. In theory he wanted to control himself more. The irony was the breathing exercises and meditative phrases just made him more agitated. They reminded him of past mistakes and the prejudices he faced at Danbury. He was an outsider and always would be. Danbury Prep was an old-money school, the kind that traced its grads back through generations of the same spoiled, inbred families. These people didn't take vacations. They "summered." Mason knew he couldn't belong to their social set, but not for the reasons they thought. The other students believed their birth to rich parents made them better than Mason. And maybe on some level, they were. They'd been exposed to more culture by the time they were five than he had in his entire life. But he knew the uncomfortable feeling they had about him had nothing to do with the fact he'd never been skiing in Vail or cleansed his palate between courses with anything other than a swig of soda. They hated him because he had something they didn't, something that no amount of money could buy them. He had freedom. He didn't care what anybody thought, and that terrified them. He was unpredictable and uncontrollable.

Still, he knew he had to calm himself before he met with the dean. Mason frequently got pissed off in situations when he faced authority and he ended up in more trouble than he would have if he'd just kissed ass and apologized.

He was thinking he should just suck it up, smile, and offer to take the test again when Kaylee Abernathy walked by, clutching a binder to her chest like a shield. They briefly locked eyes before she sat a few seats down, calm and composed. Mason was pretty sure she had no concerns about an ass-reaming in her future.

He looked at her as much as he could without being obvious. Maybe it was the warm yellow of the midday sun in the hall, but he swore something about her was profoundly different from every other girl he'd ever seen. She glowed. Mason had no other way to describe it. She was pretty with her rich, brown hair and enormous eyes, but so were tons of other girls at Danbury. They all were well bred and well groomed. But Kaylee glowed. She gave off a vibe that said she wasn't someone who wasted people's time. She was serious but friendly.

To his chagrin, she didn't seem to notice him at all as she sat quietly perusing the pages in her binder.

She had noticed Mason, of course. He had unruly, dark hair and skin smooth and white like porcelain, with stormy eyes that seemed to see everything around him. She noticed him all right. Kaylee was just very good at playing cool. Mason needed to get her attention and was trying to pick a strategy to get closer to her when Glinda interrupted his thoughts.

"You're delusional," she spat out. Mason faced her. He had forgotten Glinda was even there after Kaylee walked in. "Stop drooling. You have absolutely no chance with her, or anybody like her." Glinda had nothing personal against Kaylee. She was nice in a sickeningly sweet way and had eyes so blue Glinda thought they might be tinted lenses. "She is so above your pay grade."

"You think so?" Mason knew damn well she was above his pay grade. Maybe that was part of her appeal.

"You need to understand something. There is no such thing as democracy in dating." Mason seemed to smile as Glinda spoke, and this made her even more insistent. He really was clueless. "Danbury Prep has a caste system. She is upper. You are lower. If this were India or wherever, you'd spend your life fetching water for her or scrubbing her cows or something."

"I can hear you, you know," Kaylee said loudly. Mason fell for her even harder in that moment.

"Go ahead. Make a play for her," Glinda kept on going. She didn't care who heard. "I'll remind you of our little chat when you're getting your ass kicked by a bunch of jocks who think you're trespassing on their territory."

Mason was smart enough to know she was right. But he was also dumb enough to ignore her. She was about to say something else when a teacher appeared in the hallway. "I believe you're supposed to be in English Lit right now, Ms. Adams."

Glinda took her time walking away. She shot a final warning to him about Kaylee. "I hope she's worth it."

Mason hoped he had the chance to find out. When he and Kaylee were finally alone, he was trying to figure out what exactly to say to her.

"She's wrong, you know," she spoke first.

"About my career as a cow scrubber?"

Kaylee smiled and shook her head. "No, about you getting your ass kicked by a bunch of jocks."

"You're not their territory?"

"They wouldn't risk kicking anybody's ass. They're too worried about messing up their scholarship chances."

They sat silently for a moment as Mason was trying hard to think of something clever to say back to her. It usually came so easily to him, but she was seriously jamming his brainwaves. He had to say something, so he went for the obvious. "What are you in for?" He gestured to the dean's door, hating how it sounded the second it came out of his mouth. "I'm showing the dean some designs for the new cheerleading uniforms." She raised her notebook. "What about you?"

"Same," Mason replied, stone faced. "I really hope he goes for the pleated skirt. It has so much more bounce to it." He grinned and thought he caught a tiny smile at the corner of her eye, but he wasn't sure. Maybe he'd gone too far.

"You're making fun of me," she said.

"I thought I was having fun with you."

She considered this like she wasn't sure she agreed. Mason was afraid he was losing her. "Einarson thinks I cheated on my Calc test."

"Why?"

"Because I got a perfect score." He didn't add that usually he intentionally got one or two wrong just to keep the teachers off his back. They were always keeping a suspicious eye on him. The Calc test had been too easy. He couldn't bring himself to fake mistakes.

"That's not exactly proof you cheated," Kaylee remarked. "What do they think they can do to you for that?"

"Torture, waterboarding. That sort of thing."

That got a smile out of her.

"Ms. Abernathy? Dean Van de Sant is ready for you." The voice startled them out of the moment. Kaylee stood, but Mason reached out toward her. He didn't want to let her go. She had responded differently than any other person at the school would've when she heard his story.

"Wait."

She turned and looked at him, raising an eyebrow as if to say, *Well?*

"Why didn't you ask if I did it?"

"Did what?" She looked confused.

"Cheated," Mason said. "Why didn't you ask if I cheated on the test?"

Kaylee grinned. "I don't think you did. You're smarter than you let on."

With that, she was gone and Mason was smitten.

4.BRACES AND FIRST BRAS

"He pursued her at first. It was very sweet."

Keesha sat straight in her chair, calm and confident. She smoothed her plaid uniform skirt across her thighs. She had a natural desire to help the police. They were the good guys after all. But she wasn't sure exactly why they wanted to know about Mason and Kaylee's relationship. Word had spread that a police car had shown up at the Abernathy residence. Mason and Kaylee hadn't come to school that day so rumors were flying about them running away. Keesha thought it was possible, but she wasn't sure she should help the authorities. If Kaylee ran away, maybe she didn't want to be found.

Keesha would never run away herself, of course, though she fantasized about it sometimes. She thought about withdrawing all the money from her allowance account and using it to get by; she knew from television shows not to use a credit card because police could track her. She'd go to some small town in a state with a good cheap public university system. She would be running away, not throwing her life away. She'd enroll in a high school and maybe get a job as a waitress somewhere. She was very good at remembering lists and things.

If she did run away, she'd want her friends to cover for her.

"How did Mason treat Kaylee?" the younger detective asked. Keesha thought he was cute. He seemed so businesslike. This was probably a small case for the police but he was acting as professionally as if it were a very serious crime they were investigating.

"Mason is crazy about her." The cops clearly thought Mason was the mastermind of whatever had happened. It didn't surprise Keesha. "I know he has the reputation of being some sort of bad boy, but he's so much more than that. He's gentle. And kind. And decent."

"No one else has called him gentle."

"You know about the roses, right?" Keesha told them about Mason's first overture to Kaylee. "He planted rose petals in her locker that spilled out when she opened it, like something from a movie."

Keesha knew any boy who could plan something like that couldn't be bad deep down. Her heart fluttered a little at the thought of it. She herself didn't date. She didn't have time to. Her days were spent studying and leading the various clubs on campus. Keesha wanted to get into Dartmouth and realized she needed more help than most of her classmates because they were legacies. Their parents and grandparents had gone to Ivy League schools. They had given so much money to the colleges over the years that they had entire buildings named after them. Keesha's parents were extremely successful, but they had attended state schools for both undergrad and medical schools. They could provide the best money could buy, but they couldn't open doors at the Ivies.

They didn't realize the pressure Keesha felt. "Go out and have fun," her parents were always telling her. Fun was something she'd have later. Boys fell into that category; right now they would just waste her precious time.

Kaylee didn't have such worries. She could go anywhere she wanted based on her family name alone. Keesha wasn't jealous as she'd been Kaylee's best friend for years. They'd been through braces and first bras together. They'd giggled over Judy Blume books, eager to see what the big fuss about "womanhood" was all about. But after she finally started getting her period a few years ago, Kaylee seemed to withdraw into herself a little, like it was a disappointment after all the hoopla. The change in her was subtle, but Keesha knew it was there. Kaylee wasn't entirely comfortable in her body, fantastic as it was.

"So you think Mason was good for Kaylee?" The older detective seemed skeptical.

"You have to understand, when Mason started dating Kaylee, she was happier than she had been in a very long time. She smiled more than she had in years."

"So she wasn't bothered by his getting into the fight with Jared? Or getting in trouble with his teachers?"

"Of course she didn't want him to fight, or get in trouble, but she could see past that." Keesha felt defensive. "I know you want to believe that Mason was a bad influence on Kaylee, but I am telling you, he was anything but that."

Though now she wondered about the rose petals in Kaylee's locker. How had Mason gotten past the lock to put them there?

5. THE FIRST KISS

Mason watched from a distance as Kaylee and Keesha walked down the hall chatting happily. He thought he'd heard one of them say something about a new cheer. He never thought of himself as someone who would fall for a cheerleader. The word alone made him cringe. Nothing about leading cheers or being cheerful appealed to him, but here he was making a bold overture to the cocaptain of the varsity squad.

The hallway was swarming with students. Jared Slater was handing out flyers for the student body election and shaking hands with people, like he was a politician out doing some old-timey stumping. If there was a baby within fifty yards, Jared would find it and kiss it.

When Kaylee opened her locker, a carefully rigged shelf loaded with red rose petals tilted forward, sending them cascading down, fluttering to the floor. It had taken Mason forever to rig the locker just right so the petals fluttered and didn't just dump down in one big lump. Luckily he had free rein of the building after hours thanks to his father's master keys. He had stripped every red rose in the school's garden to get enough petals.

Mason felt oddly calm as he watched Kaylee. He didn't know her, but he knew she'd like what he'd done. When she opened the locker, he slipped across the hall and stood next to the open door. When she closed it, he was there, looking calm and in control.

"I swear you won't regret me," was all he could think of to say. He knew she must have a million reasons to say no to him. He was a working-class kid who got into trouble all the time. He couldn't treat her to the fancy restaurants and ski vacations like other guys at Danbury could. They had almost nothing in common other than both attending the same school. He had little to offer her except his intense devotion.

"I never do anything I'd regret," Kaylee whispered. That simple. She didn't hesitate. She didn't know him at all, but she felt the connection too. So Mason kissed her. He didn't think about it. He didn't debate it. He just did it. And she kissed back. He felt the hallway around them grow silent as other students realized what was happening.

Jared Slater watched from a distance, his heart sinking as the irresponsible hothead Mason Henry kissed his ex-girlfriend. It devastated him, but, of course, Jared kept his heartache to himself. Now here she was in this very public display of affection with someone Jared was superior to on every level. He was better-looking, smarter, more polished, came from a better family, and was more popular. Jared had never felt so much aching and anger at the same time.

He watched as their kiss lingered way too long before they reluctantly pulled away from each other. Mason gently closed her locker and then took Kaylee by the hand and led her through the crowd of students and out the door of the school.

Outside, Mason guided Kaylee to his beat-up Toyota Corolla and opened the door for her to get in. Kaylee had never felt so charged in all her life. She'd swear she could feel the breeze on each hair on her arms and smell the different types of trees around them.

She had no idea where he was taking her, but at that point, she would have gone anywhere with him.

The car interior was like nothing Kaylee had ever seen before. It was an economy model. There was no fabric or leather trim on the doors, just a bare factory metal. The passenger-side floor was brown with rust and gray duct tape was wrapped around the steering wheel. Kaylee half expected Mason to get out and push the car to get it started.

"I know it's a piece of crap," he said as he slid into the driver's seat. "But it gets me where I need to go."

"No, it's fine." Kaylee smiled reassuringly at him. "I've had my tetanus shot."

Mason grinned. He reached over to get her seat belt, letting his hand come very close to her breast as he pulled it across her, without ever touching it. He snapped it with a loud *CLICK*, and then leaned over and kissed her again.

Kaylee could not believe she was doing this. Her parents would freak. Her sister, Anne, would freak. Everyone she knew back at the school was probably already freaking. She could hear the ping of her phone repeatedly as people texted her, but instead of reading them, she turned the phone off. Mason smiled approval and took her hand as they pulled out of the parking lot.

"Are you okay with going for a ride?" he asked. Kaylee nodded. She was already on the most exciting ride of her life.

They drove in silence for what seemed like forever, first on the main business road as it exited the town, then as it became more rural and they found themselves passing farm after farm.

"Look, there's a cow scrubber." Those were the first words Mason said in over fifteen minutes and Kaylee laughed out loud. She had replayed the conversation from the first time they met over and over again in her head, trying to discern if there was a hint of a message in their banter. She realized the message was not in the words, but in the very fact that Mason had engaged her. He flirted. It was something he ordinarily didn't do, and certainly hadn't done with anyone else at Danbury.

Eventually they entered another city. Curiosity overcame her and she finally asked what they were doing. The "what" seemed more important somehow than the "where."

"I'm taking you to my all-time favorite place for lunch," Mason said.

"You mean it's better than the cafeteria food?"

"Barely, but it's got better ambiance."

Soon, they were in the heart of a typical northeastern urban town. Dreary brick buildings pushed against the sidewalks with very little greenery in sight. Hand-painted signs advertised the shoe repair shops, dry cleaners, and hair salons within. Chain stores with their bright signs and crisp exteriors had not infiltrated yet. Kaylee drank it all in. "So this is what they call ambiance?"

Mason pulled the car over in front of a tiny Italian restaurant.

"Did we just drive for an hour and a half to eat pizza?" Kaylee asked.

Mason nodded. "You'll see."

He led her inside. Brown paneling went halfway up the walls and red flocked wallpaper covered the rest. The second they stepped inside, someone yelled. "Get the hell out of my place, you greasy punk." Kaylee cringed.

From out of nowhere, a burly old man in a soiled white apron grabbed Mason in a huge hug. "You think you're too good to come around here for a slice? They got you eating pizza with arugula and goat cheese on it up at that place?"

"Arugula? Goat cheese? Are you kidding me? Never," Mason said. The old man grunted approval, and with impeccable timing, Mason added, "I prefer pesto and caramelized onions."

The man smacked the back of Mason's head. "Always a mouth." He seemed to notice Kaylee for the first time and addressed her directly.

"Did he kidnap you? Because I know sure as hell that he couldn't get a girl as pretty as you without drugging her or some such nonsense."

"Jesus, Babe. Really?" Mason shook his head. "I haven't drugged anyone in weeks."

"I am here of my own free will," Kaylee assured the man. "But thanks for the tip. From now on I will not let any drink I have out of my sight when I'm with him."

Babe smiled broadly. "Smart cookie."

"Kaylee Abernathy, meet Babe DiLuca." Kaylee held out her hand to shake as Mason introduced them, and Babe made a gallant show of kissing it.

Mason rolled his eyes.

From out of the back of the kitchen came a loud shriek. Babe looked at Mason. In unison, they said. "Here we go."

A tiny woman with an enormous nest of black hair came barreling toward them. A customer on his way to the exit nearly jumped out of her way. "I thought I recognized that voice!" She grabbed Mason by both arms and hugged him hard, impaling him on her disproportionately large breasts. As soon as she pulled away, her tone changed to one of complete annoyance. "You don't call. You don't write." She gestured to Kaylee. "Next I know you'll be married without inviting me to the wedding. Shame on you."

"Kaylee, meet Diane DiLuca. I worked here for Diane and Babe from the time I was twelve until we moved away last year," Mason explained.

Diane harrumphed when he said that. "Worked? He ate is what he did best." She took a good look at Kaylee. "I look at your bony arms and all I can think is, 'Someone feed that poor thing.' You should be in a commercial with flies all over your face."

Mason smiled at Kaylee. "She means that in the nicest way possible."

"Don't get me wrong." Diane squeezed Kaylee's shoulders. "You're beautiful like a model. But you know why those women on the runways never smile? They're starving. They haven't had a nice slice since they hit puberty."

"I am starving," Kaylee replied. "Would you mind terribly if

I had something to eat here?" She knew exactly what she was doing. Mason enjoyed the show.

A huge smile spread across Diane's face. "Can you get something to eat? Can she get something to eat? I like this girl. Mason, you better not mess this up. Skinny girl, you sit. I'll give you food."

Mason guided Kaylee to a red vinyl booth and Babe made a show of lighting the candle on the table before stepping away. "I'll leave you two alone."

Kaylee grinned.

"I'm guessing I don't need a menu."

Mason shook his head. "You'll be getting everything on the menu."

"Those people love you."

"It's mutual."

Mason reached over and took Kaylee's hands. "I'm glad you're here with me."

"I can't think of anyplace else I'd rather be right now." It was true. Kaylee felt so content at the moment that anything stressful in her life seemed far away and unimportant.

"Danbury must seem so sterile to you compared to here." She looked around. Several of the booths were patched with duct tape, but someone had taken the time to use red magic marker to color them in so the patches would at least match the vinyl. A crucifix hung on the wall behind the cash register.

"Not sterile exactly. There's a fair share of personalities there. Glinda. Trevor."

"I've known Trevor since forever," Kaylee said. "He's like a brother to me."

"I think people at Danbury have personalities, they're just trained not to show too much of them. You're all judged if you don't follow the rules."

"I'm sure this place has rules too," Kaylee reasoned. She felt herself getting a little defensive. She knew Danbury had its faults, but it was her school.

"No, it doesn't," Mason asserted.

"Oh, I'm sure it does."

"People accept people here."

"So if I wear an Eagles jersey, they'll be fine with that?"

"Eagles? Of course not."

"Or if I request a gluten-free pizza?"

Mason cringed a little. "Keep your voice down when you say that. Seriously. Somebody asked for vegetarian sausage once. It wasn't pretty."

"See? You have rules. Weird rules, but rules."

"Point taken." He nodded. "But I think people accept flaws more here."

"But being gluten-free isn't a flaw?"

"You said that, I didn't. I think you have to be mentally ill to give up real bread and pasta and pizza."

"So I made my point."

"Okay, there are rules here. But people are also allowed to have feelings."

"We have feelings at Danbury."

"No, you don't." Mason shook his head. "Not like here or a lot of other places."

"Like you could start crying in front of Babe?"

"No, he would call me a pussy." Mason realized as he said the last word that it was perhaps too coarse. "I'm sorry. I meant to say he would make fun of me."

"So? How is that allowing you to have feelings?"

"If I cried in front of Diane, she'd hug me. There's nobody at Danbury who would hug anybody. It's like hugs are for poor people."

"I think that was a slogan of a fund-raiser we had in the third grade. Hugs for the Poor."

Mason smiled. "Yeah?"

As they talked, a twentysomething guy walked by the table. Kaylee shook her head in a bit of amusement.

"What's funny?" Mason asked.

"That guy just winked at me," Kaylee said. "I didn't know guys still winked."

"Who? That guy?" Mason whipped around in his seat. He saw the culprit at the counter waiting for his pizza. Mason stood up.

"What are you doing?" Kaylee asked.

But Mason didn't answer. He strode over to the guy. "Did you wink at my date?"

"No, of course not." The guy sensed trouble. He stiffened and his eyes went to the door, like he wanted to bolt.

"So you're saying she's a liar?"

"No! Of course not."

"Mason, what are you doing? It's no big deal," Kaylee was next to him by now, clearly alarmed.

Mason pushed the guy's chest, forcing him back against the counter. "Which one is it? Did you do it, or are you calling her a liar?"

Kaylee took a step toward them, but Mason held out a finger to stop her.

"Which one is it?" Mason repeated. "Did you wink at her, or are you calling her a liar?"

The guy stared at Mason, and then at Kaylee, considering his next move. By this time, Diane and Babe had come out from the kitchen. Diane eyeballed the scene but didn't intervene.

"I did it. I'm sorry," the guy said. "It won't happen again."

When Mason released the guy, he took off for the door.

Mason turned to Kaylee. "That was intense." She said it with as little judgment as possible, but the truth was, she was shaken.

"It's okay," Mason assured her. "I had to do that. It's just the way things work around here."

"So he broke some sort of rule?"

"I see where you're going with this." Mason smiled.

"I'm just trying to be clear," Kaylee said. "You don't exactly have rules here, but you were mad at him for not following the rules you don't have?"

Mason smiled. "Exactly."

"I just wanted to be clear." Kaylee wasn't sure what had just happened, but she knew she had never had anyone defend her like that before. His reaction had scared her a little, but it also thrilled her.

They sat back in their booth. Diane brought out enough food to feed ten people. Kaylee welcomed the distraction. She inhaled the aroma. "This is unbelievable. Thank you." Diane grinned. "You have to eat it. All of it."

She tried it all. Mason explained the various dishes, how Babe made some of the pastas himself and how Diane added a pinch of sugar to almost everything she made. "She says it's because she wants everybody to know she's sweet, but really, it cuts the acid of the tomatoes."

He and Kaylee ate like a comfortable couple. At one point Mason wiped the corner of her mouth with his finger. She grinned. "You just cleaned my face."

"What was I supposed to do? It was dirty."

By the time the meal was over, Kaylee felt like she could not eat again for a week. Diane still insisted on wrapping all the leftovers up to take with them, and gave some fresh food for Mason's father. She hugged them good-bye like they were soldiers going off to war.

They rode back through the countryside in silence. When Mason pulled up to her house and walked her to the door, it was almost seven. She knew her father was probably waiting for her, so their good-bye was more rushed than she'd have liked.

"Thank you. That was some day," she whispered as she gently kissed his lips.

Mason nodded. "There's more where that came from."

He started walking away but then turned back. "I have something you should know. I'm not proud of it."

Kaylee waited.

"I really do like pizza with pesto and caramelized onions."

6.BUGGED

"How can I help you gentlemen?" Jared Slater, senior class president, sat across from the detectives. "I'm happy to answer any questions you have. Think of me as a liaison between you and the Danbury Prep community. I make it my business to know everything that goes on in this school."

Without taking his eyes off them, he slipped a hand under the table and planted a tiny electronic device—a bug. Jared wasn't kidding about knowing everything that went on in the school. These interrogations would be no exception.

"I understand you want to know about Mason and Kaylee. There's not much to know. She came to her senses and broke up with him last night at Keesha's party. Everyone saw it."

"Tell us about the party," the younger detective prodded.

"It was typical. Almost everybody there was from Danbury. Keesha was doing the hostess thing like she does. People were drinking." He paused, concern spreading on his brow. "You're not going to inform our parents about this, are you?"

The older detective shook his head. "We only care about Mason and Kaylee."

"Kaylee showed up to the party alone. That in itself was rare. Since she and Mason started dating a few months back he didn't let her out of his sight. He's the jealous type. He smothered her."

But last night she was solo and Jared decided to talk to her. Kaylee had been rushing through the party and he stepped in front of her. She was startled at first, but then she smiled. He'd always liked her smile. When they were dating, he'd told her she didn't smile often enough. But she smiled when she saw him last night. He took that as a good sign.

"You surprised me."

"You look great," he'd told her. Some guys hesitated to do that sort of thing, but Jared knew girls liked to be complimented. And she did look great. She always did.

"Um. Thanks." She looked over his shoulder. Jared knew Kaylee probably was worried Mason would see them talking and get angry.

"I told her she could always come to me if she needed anything," Jared continued telling the detectives. "I think I sensed something. I've been worried about her ever since she started dating Mason."

"Worried how?" the older detective asked.

"People will tell you that I'm bitter that Kaylee ended up with Mason, but that's not true." He knew it was a little true, but the detectives didn't need to know that because he was genuinely concerned. "I was disturbed she ended up with Mason because Mason is volatile and Kaylee is vulnerable."

"Vulnerable is a strong word."

"I feel strongly about it. She's lived a very sheltered life. She has no idea what kind of trouble somebody like Mason can get into."

"I take it you know." The older detective seemed skeptical.

"Here's what you need to understand about Mason Henry. He thinks people don't like him because he's poor, because we're all such snobs that we can't tolerate someone who's different than we are. But people don't like Mason because he's unlikable. It's that simple. He's never learned to play well with others, as my mother would say."

"What makes him 'unlikable'?"

Jared thought about this a moment. He knew his answer would reveal as much about his own personality as it would Mason's. "We all have opinions, and we have learned how to share them in a way so as not to offend whenever possible. Obviously, sometimes a leader needs to step up and voice an opinion that's unpopular if it's for the greater good, but he does not have to say it in a way that's insulting. Mason doesn't realize that. Everything he says comes out like an insult. He could say hello aggressively. He wants to be an outsider. He flaunts it."

"So it's just a personality conflict between you? Nothing more?"

Jared shook his head. "I know how it looks to you. I know I'm the ex-boyfriend, but I am not some fool trying to get back at his girlfriend's new boyfriend. It's serious. I think Mason may have gotten rough with Kaylee."

This got the detectives' attention. "What do you mean, 'rough'?"

"You know, abusive."

"We're listening."

"I saw something, evidence, about a month ago during the school elections."

It had been a tight race between Jared and Keesha and he was out trying to drum up support. Jared knew he was clearly a better candidate with a very good relationship with students and faculty alike, but Keesha had leadership roles in practically every club on campus and she was parlaying that exposure into votes.

"I was handing out flyers between classes. I'd gone with a simple 'Vote for Jared' motif on my campaign materials." Jared thought the red, white, and blue flyers harkened back to an earlier time when the political landscape was not so corrupt. His grandfather had been a state senator and Jared also hoped to hold a national office one day. "I really think we as a country need to start bringing honest campaigning back into the election process."

"You were telling us about the abuse?"

"Of course. I saw Kaylee in the hall. I could tell something was off about her," Jared continued. "And sure enough when she got close, I saw the bruises on her arms. Small ones, the size of coins. Or fingerprints. They looked like someone had grabbed her. I asked her about them and she said she'd fallen into a coat hook by her front door. I knew a coat hook couldn't make marks like that."

His concern was already mounting when Mason strutted up, cocky as always. It hit him how those bruises got there. WHO had caused those bruises. He wasn't sure what came over him, but he grabbed Mason.

"What did you do to her?"

"What do you mean?" Mason asked, confused. His innocent act made Jared even angrier.

"What did you do to her, you prick?" Jared pulled on Kaylee's arm to show Mason the bruises. When Mason stepped back Jared dropped Kaylee's arm and got nose to nose with him. "You should've seen the look on his face. Pure fear. I'm bigger and stronger than he is, and I was clearly not backing down. His type relies heavily on intimidation, and I was not intimidated."

"So you beat him up?"

"Of course not. I'd taken karate for six years with Sensei Enkoji. I used some of my skills and pinned him. I wanted to diffuse a potentially bad situation. If I'd wanted to do more, I could've. I want to be clear that I'm not usually someone who resorts to that kind of rough behavior," he shifted in his chair. "But I had to stand up for Kaylee."

It was risky to get in a fight so close to the election. Fighting was hardly presidential behavior, but his emotions got the better of him. He wasn't sure the fight would dissuade Mason from doing anything, but he knew how to get rid of him with a phone call.

But that hadn't worked out either and Jared was still trying to figure out why.

His father had called the dean about the fight and by all rights Mason should have been expelled. Dean Van de Sant said as much when the two men spoke. But he quickly changed his tune after talking to Mason's dad, Mike Henry, the school's janitor and all-around tradesman. Van de Sant refused to say any more about it, only that Mason deserved a second chance.

Jared knew something else was in play. He prided himself in keeping on top of all the gossip of the school. Information was power. He'd even installed several cameras and audio transmitters around the Danbury campus to capture things that could be useful to him and consequently had footage of just about every indiscretion he could think of: makeout sessions in closets, rainbow parties in the locker room, upperclassmen bullying the unders, teachers stealing from student lockers, honor students cheating on exams. Jared found it amazing how people were willing to do just about anything to keep their secrets hidden. He had a personal standard for himself not to do or say anything he wouldn't want the world to know about. Everyone, he believed, should live like that. And if they didn't, well, why shouldn't he benefit? Society seemed so concerned about the increasing lack of privacy, but Jared welcomed it. People would behave better, he believed, if they realized they were being watched.

When it became clear he was going to lose the election to Keesha, Jared knew he had to do something to prevent someone unworthy from taking charge of the student government. So he arranged a private meeting with her in the student government office. She'd resisted at first. She thought he was going to try to enlist her help in winning Kaylee back, or was going to ask her out. Of course both were ridiculous. She realized he would do neither as soon as she saw the image on his open laptop, with the camera frozen on the second-floor girls' bathroom. She sat without speaking as he hit PLAY and showed her footage of her entering the bathroom, digging through her purse, and swallowing a handful of pills.

Now for all he knew at the time, they may have been antibiotics or ibuprofen. But when Keesha saw herself in grainy black and white, her face turned ashen. Jared realized he'd struck gold. She resigned from the race the next day, citing time issues. With his primary competitor gone, Jared won by a landslide. He was now Jared Slater, student body president.

Information was power. Knowledge was power. Jared Slater had power.

And that was why he was so frustrated about Mason. Somehow he had escaped punishment for the fight in the hallway and Jared didn't know why. Now the police were here asking about him. He hoped she was okay.

"You need to find them," he said. "If Kaylee is with Mason, she's not safe."

7. I WON'T BE YOUR FIRST

Mason and Kaylee lay on a rough Navajo-print blanket at the park, staring up at the clouds. It was one of those perfect warm days that seemed like a gift, with white pillows gently blowing across azure-blue skies. It was the rare Saturday afternoon when Kaylee didn't have any cheerleading responsibilities and they could spend the entire day together. The park was crowded with people, but Kaylee and Mason had found an isolated corner to stretch out.

"You really see an elephant?" Mason tilted his head back and forth, squinting, trying to spot what Kaylee saw.

"I can't believe you don't see an elephant. There's the tusk. And the giant ears," Kaylee said. Mason shook his head. She pointed to another spot. "Look, over there, a heart. A big one. It looks like it has the letters *M* and *K* in it."

"I think you're making this stuff up."

"Probably."

Mason rolled over to his side and kissed her slowly and sweetly. It grew more urgent before he pulled away.

"I know you want to go farther." Kaylee played with a blade of grass as she spoke.

Mason shook his head. "I'm not going to pressure you."

"I know. I know you're not," she said. "I'm not saying you are."

"We can wait."

"I know we can, but why should we?"

"Let's talk about this in a month."

"No. We need to talk about it now," she insisted. "I feel like an idiot. It's just sex. It's not a big deal."

"Yeah. It actually is. Or it will be with us."

"You know what I mean." She draped an arm over his chest. "I'm like, the only one who hasn't had sex."

"You've been hanging around with Lily for too long."

Mason wasn't sure how to proceed. He wanted to rip Kaylee's clothes off every time they were together, but he knew this was a big deal and he didn't want to screw it up. People remember their first time. He was honored she wanted him to be her first, but he wasn't sure she wanted to for the right reasons. Doing it because everybody else was doing it was the worst reason he could think of, and he was worried she would freak out afterward and want to break up.

Kaylee interrupted his thoughts. "I won't be your first, will I?"

Mason dreaded this kind of talk. He knew that it never led to anything good, but also knew that if he tried to stop, even more trouble would follow.

"Why do you want to know things that will upset you?" If he knew the answer to that question, he realized, he would be one of the smartest guys in the world. Or at least, the luckiest, so he wouldn't have to have these kinds of conversations again.

"I'm a girl. And I need to know."

He paused before he answered. "No. You won't be my first."

Kaylee felt herself deflate a little. She knew she wouldn't be, but she'd still hoped he hadn't ever cared that much for anyone else. "Who was she?"

"I'm not going to tell you that."

"Oh my God. Do I know her?" Her mind flashed to Lily. She had more conquests than the Roman Empire.

"No. You do not know her. I just don't want to go there. It's a private thing. If we do it . . ."

"When we do it." Kaylee interrupted him.

". . . when we do it, I won't tell that to anybody either." Mason brushed some hair away from her eyes.

"You're supposed to be a gentleman where I'm concerned, but not anybody else." She was trying to be cute and still get her point across. Mason played along.

"Right. I see what you mean."

"It makes sense to me."

"I can see why."

Kaylee stared at him seriously. "You're not going to tell me, are you?"

Mason shook his head. "I'm sorry."

Kaylee sat up. "You're being a gentleman."

"I'm trying."

"I like you for the same reason I'm annoyed with you."

"I have that effect on people." He pointed upward. "Look! A cloud that's shaped like, what's that word? A cloud."

Kaylee smacked his chest. He pulled her back down to the blanket. "Will I be your second?"

Jesus, Mason thought. She should work for the Stasi interrogating people. "No."

"How many? Fourth? Fifth? Twentieth?" she asked.

"Third. You'd be my third. But you'll be the first I actually love."

8. AN ACTIONABLE INCIDENT

Van de Sant refused to sit in front of the detectives to be interrogated like a common criminal. He was allowing them to use *his* faculty lounge, and they should be respectful enough to be forthcoming about why they were there.

"If Danbury students are in some sort of trouble, I need to know about it," he told them. "Parents need to be notified. We have some very important people in our school community, and they expect to be kept apprised of any situation."

What he meant was people were going to start calling him for information, and if he didn't provide it, they would think he wasn't doing his job. And if they thought he wasn't doing his job, they'd fire him. These were not loyal people, at least not to their employees. They were people who were accustomed to getting what they wanted. They would not care that he'd been at Danbury for twenty years. They would just say he had passed his prime and needed to move on. In his experience millionaires were not tolerant of anything that caused them discomfort, even mental discomfort. Waiting for information counted.

"I'm aware that Kaylee Abernathy and Mason Henry were

absent from school today. Our very active student gossip mill reports they ran away. Is this true?"

The detectives shared a quick glance before the older one spoke. "At this point, we can't elaborate on what we're investigating."

"This is just standard procedure," the younger one added. "You'll be kept in the loop when we're ready to create a loop."

The dean nodded, not remotely mollified. "Would police be involved if they'd simply run away?"

"Clearly, you are savvy enough to understand this is not an ordinary situation," the younger detective answered. "But that's all I can tell you."

That was more like it. "I'm not surprised. Trouble follows Mason."

"How exactly?" the older detective asked.

"You have to understand that Mason is not like other students here at Danbury. He's here because his father works in the main-tenance department. We offer free tuition to the children of any school employees who can pass the entrance exam and maintain their grades." Van de Sant refused to use the word "scholarship," as that implied extraordinary talent or intelligence. These students simply had to meet the normal requirements.

"So he's a smart kid?"

"He passed the entrance test."

"How hard was that to do?"

"He was the first child of someone not in the administrative or faculty side of things to do so."

"So the answer is yes. He is a smart kid."

"He meets the entrance requirements. One could argue that implies a baseline intelligence." Van de Sant hated to give any credit to the cocky pissant. The rules about passing the entrance test and maintaining grades were designed specifically to keep up the appearance of being an equal-opportunity educator. No one had expected anyone related to a laborer at the school to actually succeed at gaining admission. Common sense dictated the economic and cultural differences alone would make it an ill fit.

"How was he 'not like other students'?" the younger detective pushed. "Besides what his father did for a living?"

Van de Sant was thoroughly annoyed by the subtext of the question. The detective thought snobbery was the reason he disliked Mason when that clearly wasn't the case. He himself had been the son of a working-class man. His father had been a house painter who taught him the importance of hard work and knowing your place. He credited his father with instilling him with an eye for detail and appreciation of things being done the right way.

"Mason is intelligent, as I said. He surprised his teachers in that regard, but he's also disrespectful. I've received numerous complaints about him questioning his teachers' mastery of their subjects and disrupting class with his insistence on debating every little point. A few teachers enjoy what they consider academic enthusiasm, but most find him arrogant. I'm constantly soothing egos and calming tempers where Mason is concerned."

"Is he usually right?" the older detective asked.

"Right about what?"

"When he questions his teachers. Was he usually right?"

"That's not the point. If he's making enemies of his teachers, he's clearly wrong. That, sir, is a life lesson everyone should learn. He may have won the occasional battle, but if you'll pardon my alteration of the expression, he put himself in the middle of wars."

He'd wished he'd had a way to punish Mason and get him to curtail his rants, but the boy had always managed to stop just shy of breaking a rule or somehow avoiding detection. He'd been accused of cheating on a Calculus test and taken a harder one. He got a perfect score.

"We understand Mason was in a fight not too long ago."

Van de Sant nodded. When the fight with Jared Slater happened, the dean had been glad. He finally had an actionable incident to get rid of what he thought of as a bad seed. Of course, it didn't work out the way he'd hoped.

"What's the standard punishment for fighting on campus?"

"There is no standard punishment at Danbury." Van de Sant

knew they were trying to corner him into saying Mason got special treatment. "We are a private academy, not a public school with a huge list of arbitrary state rules. We realize that every incident has extenuating circumstances. Two years ago a student was acting out and we realized his mother was sick. Of course we treated that differently than someone acting out for no reason."

"So were there extenuating circumstances with Mason?"

"Not anything quite so dramatic as a mother with cancer."

"Then what was it?"

"There was nothing specific, if that's what you're looking for." He knew he couldn't answer honestly. "In that particular case, I considered the options and meted out what I thought was the appropriate punishment. I felt that cooler heads should prevail and he should be given a second chance."

Van de Sant had been determined to expel him, but Mason's father had proven a worthy opponent. He had information about him that Van de Sant did not want to become public. He promised it would not as long as Mason was a student at Danbury. It was blackmail, pure and simple. Van de Sant respected that.

"Trust me, when I heard this morning that he and Kaylee were in some sort of situation, it gave me great pause. I would hate to have allowed someone violent to remain in the school and jeopardize other students."

9.DID I HURT YOU?

Mason watched as Kaylee read a book on the grass. A fly was bothering her and she was swatting at it with an irritated look on her face that was nothing short of, dare he say it, cute. She held very still, willing the fly to land on her book. When it did, she quickly slammed the book shut. It caught some of her hair, but not the fly.

Mason handed Kaylee a soda and stretched out next to her. He had started to think of this spot in the park as their spot. It was far enough away from the crowds so as to feel private, but still public enough for good people watching. Kaylee ordinarily would be gazing at the families in the playground nearby or at the old people feeding birds from the park benches, wondering what their lives were like. She'd create stories about them, like the elderly couple with twelve grown kids who told them they had to downsize to a smaller home for financial reasons but really just wanted to make sure no one could ever move back in with them. Or the young couple who were planning to elope because the guy was going off to study in another country and they wanted to make sure she could go with him, or the pregnant woman terrified she was carrying a baby from a one-night stand she'd had when she was mad at her boyfriend.

But Kaylee had been quiet today. Not pouty or anything, just not really into interacting with him. He felt horrible. They'd had sex, or made love, or whatever it was, the week before and they hadn't really talked about it since. It hadn't gone as expected, and he wasn't sure how to proceed. He realized he needed to end this limbo and knocked on her book like he was knocking on a door.

"Anybody there?"

"Nobody's home," she teased.

"My car broke down and I need to use the phone. Please. I swear I'm totally legit."

"Use your cell. This isn't 1975."

"Seriously, Kaylee. Put down the book."

The tone in his voice hit her. She closed the book and looked at him, dreading whatever it was he had to say.

"Are you okay?" He took her hand and stared at it deeply, studying the lines on her palm, not wanting to scare her by peering into her eyes as much as he wanted to.

"I'm fine."

"I'm sorry."

"For what?"

"You know for what. The other night."

"You didn't do anything wrong."

"I know. It's just. You seemed unhappy." Unhappy didn't quite capture it. Mason knew it might be emotional for her, for him too in a different way, but he didn't expect her to withdraw like she did. He thought it went pretty well, but she was uncharacteristically quiet afterward.

"I wasn't unhappy. I swear."

He lowered his voice. "Did I hurt you?"

"No. Yes. A little, but that's not it."

"Then what?"

"It was just a big deal."

"I know. I tried to make it special."

"You did. I'm screwing this up for you." Kaylee felt terrible. The last thing she wanted was for her own mental bullshit to make Mason feel bad.

"Just tell me what I can do."

"You didn't do anything wrong."

"Then why are you crying?"

Kaylee hadn't realized she was until he said that. She wiped her face and looked at her hand. "I'm not. Not really."

"You were that night."

"It's just a big deal. Okay? It was special. The flowers. The music. You were gentle."

"You know I love you." He pulled her into his arms. He had no idea what the hell was going on with her. He just knew he had to fix it.

"I hope so."

They lay quietly for a bit. Neither felt a sense of resolution, though what needed resolving wasn't clear. Mason squeezed her closer to him and she nuzzled her face into his chest. The quiet was striking. Until the fly buzzed nearby, landing on Mason's cheek.

"I hate that fly," Kaylee murmured.

"Goddamn fly."

10.USING HIS WORDS

"Have you tried her house in Kennebunk? Or the cabin in Stowe? Seriously, why do you think I would know where she is? Kaylee and I haven't hung in years."

Of course, that only was technically true. Trevor and Kaylee hadn't spent much quality time together in the past few years. Gone were the dress-up sessions from their childhood, when their mothers would wait until the clock struck noon so they could open a bottle of chardonnay as their children played with the designer clothes in their closets. Trevor had always loved clothes and playing dress up. He looked a bit ethereal with jet-black hair, porcelain skin, and deep blue eyes, and even as a child he was built like a male runway model—lithe and lean. When he was very young it annoyed his mother that he refused to wear baggy shirts because he didn't like the way they made him look heavier. If he could've talked back then, he would've complained his diapers made his bottom look fat. To this day, he preferred tailored clothes that showed off his trim body. Eventually, his mother had come around and enjoyed her son's impeccable sense of style.

He and Kaylee had stopped hanging out long ago when their school groups and activities gradually separated them, but they had remained close, albeit in a more subtle way. They texted and talked regularly, but rarely got together.

They joked that they were each other's common sense. When one of them was spiraling with panic about school or feeling slighted by friends, he or she would reach out to the other to be talked down and reminded that everything would be okay. They'd had more conversations about pimples than Trevor would care to admit.

Kaylee knew she could trust him with all of her secrets. Trevor knew about the importance of keeping them. She was the first person he told about being gay, a full year before he came out to anyone else. Her reaction? "I'm glad you finally figured it out so we can talk crushes." That was so Kaylee. He was himself with her before he even knew exactly what that meant.

"Tell us what you know about Kaylee and Mason," the older detective said.

"Kaylee and Mason have always been an intense couple, but usually good intense, you know? Like 'can't live without you' intense." Trevor wasn't sure why, but knew he had to protect any secrets of hers the same way she would for him. There were so many he wasn't even sure which ones would interest them the most.

"Do you think he was violent with her?"

"I know he wasn't."

"Where do you think she got the bruises on her arm?"

"So now Jared Slater is an expert on spotting abuse?"

"You don't think she was abused?"

Trevor paused. "No."

"Then where do you think the bruises came from?"

"I think she fell into some coat hooks."

"So you believe her story?"

"Yes."

"Were you surprised she started dating him?"

"I didn't think too much about it."

How could Trevor even explain Kaylee's relationship with Mason? He suspected why she would want such a brutish thing on her side, a protector of sorts, but he had only suspicions, not facts. Explaining any of it to the police would reveal too much and possibly mark Kaylee for life. She'd always seemed to be looking forward to a day when Danbury was in her rearview mirror and didn't want anything of her time there to stick with her. She yearned for a clean slate. It was partly why Trevor was concerned about her running away. No matter what happened, this was a big enough incident that it would become part of her story. When people talked of her in the future they'd certainly bring up that she was that girl who ran away with the boy from the wrong side of the tracks. For that reason alone he knew she must have had a very good reason to flee. And if she had a good reason to do it, Trevor had a good reason to protect it.

So he stuck to the basics when he talked to the detectives and told them the kinds of things everyone would say.

"We've heard that Mason had a temper." The younger detective didn't so much ask questions as throw out statements to see how Trevor would respond. Trevor thought he might be flirting with him, but he'd been wrong in the past. A lot.

"Mason had not learned to use his words like the rest of us," Trevor explained.

Kaylee would find that assessment hilarious. Mason hadn't learned to do a lot of things like the rest of us. Using words instead of fists was one of them. It was why she liked him. Trevor hoped it hadn't backfired on her.

11.THE KID WITH THE ARM

"I told you. I'm not going to talk about it." Mason couldn't believe Kaylee was bringing this up. Why couldn't she let the past stay in the past?

They were huddled in their jackets against the cool air, sitting on the roof of the main school building, staring out over the campus and to the town beyond. Danbury Prep had the feel of a small New England college. The grounds were designed by a student of Frederick Law Olmsted's and resembled his iconic Central Park. Rolling paths meandered amid the trees and sturdy brick and stucco buildings. It had the feel of a place that had witnessed a lot of history and would survive to witness much more. Every now and then, it hit Mason that he was being given a tremendous opportunity to be here.

It would be a perfect day if the conversation with Kaylee wasn't turning out to be such a drag.

"Everybody is talking about it." Kaylee shook her head. "You need to understand that."

"They're not talking about 'it.' They're talking about me."

"They're talking about you and 'it.' The thing that got you kicked out of your last school."

"I was not kicked out."

"So they asked you to leave?"

"They did not. I'm going to tell you one thing and that's it. My father got a job at Danbury, so I came with him. Tuition is free for employee's kids. If I stayed at my last school, he would have had to pay since he wasn't working there anymore."

"What about the kid with the arm?"

"He was a fucking loser."

"You're avoiding the question."

"You didn't ask a real question." Mason had to hand it to her. She was tenacious.

"Did you break the loser's arm? Did your father look for a new job because you broke that loser's arm?"

"Jesus."

"I don't care if it's true. I just want to know if it is." That was a total lie and they both knew it. Who wouldn't care?

Kaylee was conflicted. Of course she cared, but she wouldn't break up with him if he had broken someone's arm. But she could break up with him for refusing to talk to her about it. She would not tolerate him shutting her out. They were supposed to be better than that. Better than secrets. But who was she to complain? She'd told him she was a virgin.

Mason was digging his heels in. The more he did, the more she wanted him to tell her what had happened at his last school.

The story floating around Danbury was that he'd gotten into a fight with one of the school's tougher kids and broken his arm. They said Mason did it on purpose, that he'd stretched the kid's arm over the edge of a curb and stepped on it. She did not want to believe it was true.

"I told you," Mason was repeating himself almost robotically at that point. "I'm going to say one thing. My father got a job at Danbury, so I came with him. Tuition is free for employee's kids. If I stayed at my last school, he would have had to pay since he wasn't working there anymore."

"You don't get to decide what you tell me and what you don't."

"Really? I think I do. It's my life."

"I thought I was part of it."

"You are. And you're supposed to trust me."

"Why should I trust you if you don't tell me what happened?"

"Because I'm asking you to."

"That's not good enough."

"It's going to have to be."

"So that's it? We're just done."

"I never said we were done." Mason felt a panic rising in him. He was screwed. If Kaylee knew what he'd done to that bullying prick at his last school, she'd break up with him for sure. If he didn't tell her, it seemed like she would break up with him anyway.

"But you won't tell me what happened?"

"No."

Kaylee considered him. She knew Mason had a temper, but she also knew he'd never been anything but gentle with her. She was so confused she felt like crying. He was the strongest, most decent guy she ever knew and yet he had this huge shadow hanging over him. Could she be with somebody who was capable of violence? Real violence?

Mason turned to her. His eyes were moist. She'd never seen him like that.

"Can't you judge me for how I am when I'm with you? How I am now? Can't we just be us without any of that noise?"

Kaylee wanted more than anything to exist in the moment with him, to not have anything from their day-to-day lives come creeping in to what they had. "Okay. Don't tell me about the kid with the arm. I don't need to know. But I do need to know one thing."

He waited for her to continue.

"Would you ever hurt me?"

Mason pulled her close to him. He felt like a failure. How could someone he loved so completely even ask that question? "No. I could never hurt you. Never. I'd hurt myself before I'd ever do anything to hurt you."

12. RULIET

"Do you think they pulled a Ruliet?" Glinda asked the detectives. They stared blankly at her. People did that all the time. "You know. Romeo and Juliet?"

She mimed gulping a vial of poison and then stabbing herself like the famous couple, dramatically slicing the imaginary knife through her abdomen. It was quite a performance. She resisted the urge to bow at the end. The cops were not amused, but she didn't care. She was thoroughly entertaining herself, and that's all that mattered.

Glinda thrived on being different, from her multicolor hair and wild nails to the various shades of everything she wore to liven up the boring Danbury Prep uniform. In that regard, she felt a certain kinship with Mason Henry. He was an outsider. She was an outsider. But unlike Mason, she had a typical Danbury bloodline. Her family could trace themselves back to the *Mayflower*, something her grandmother would remind her of whenever Glinda showed up in one of her more outlandish outfits. Her parents had tried cutting off her allowance to keep her from buying the giant platform shoes and spiked jewelry she loved so much, but she'd sold some of her Burberry sweaters for cash and they realized stopping her was futile. She was in a phase, they decided, and while they would never encourage it, they could tolerate it until it ended. It was an approach many of the wealthy families at Danbury took when dealing with problems. Ignore them and hope they go away. It reminded Glinda of the three monkey statues. One covered his eyes with his hands, another his mouth, and the third his ears. See no evil. Speak no evil. Hear no evil. They didn't have one for do no evil. That would have been a problem for the folks at Danbury. The thought brought her back to Mason and Kaylee.

"Okay. Maybe not Ruliet. What exactly did Mason and Kaylee do?" she asked. "Rob a liquor store? Run over a little old lady and keep going? Really, just tell me and we can get on with the questions you want me to answer."

Glinda had to admit she enjoyed being one of the handful of students getting out of class for the police questioning. It made her feel more a part of the school scene than she normally was. And these detectives were characters in themselves. The old guy looked like something out of an old cop show. He was rumpled and cranky. If they let him smoke on the Danbury campus, he'd probably be chewing on a cheap cigar. The younger detective was more yummy, but incredibly square. He had a nice haircut and good bone structure, but he reminded her of a puppy dog excited to be on a walk.

"Why do you think Mason and Kaylee were together?" the younger detective asked.

Glinda rolled her eyes. "Do you even remember high school? How does anybody get together? He thinks she's hot. She thinks they look really cute together."

But in truth, Glinda had witnessed Mason and Kaylee's first meeting and she had to admit there was a strange sort of spark. Glinda and Mason had been sitting outside the dean's office when Kaylee walked up and took a seat. Glinda could tell immediately Mason was going to make a move on her just by the way he looked at her. His tongue practically rolled out of his mouth and hit the ground like a cartoon character.

Glinda also knew any relationship between the two of them would end badly. What other way could a coupling between the janitor's son and the daughter of one of the most prominent members of the community end? With them exchanging vows in a lovely wedding on Kiawah Island? Not in this lifetime.

She warned Mason about Kaylee. Not Kaylee, in particular, but about getting involved with anyone from her social class. Basically, she warned him about getting involved with any girls at Danbury. Hell, even if he got involved with Glinda, it would have caused problems, and people had low expectations of her.

"Tell us what happened at the party last night."

"I wasn't at the party. I don't go to parties."

One of those statements was true. Glinda did not go to parties, but she was most definitely at Keesha's house the night before, just not as a regular guest. She was doing what she liked to call "blending in." It was something her mother had constantly admonished her to do. "Glinda, dear, can't you just wear a dress like every other girl at the social to blend in?" "Glinda, sweetheart, can't you let me take you to my stylist to get your hair done so you can blend in on vacation?" The answer, of course, was always, "No."

Her mother's version of blending in and her own version were very different things. When Glinda was small, her mother delighted in how her daughter stood out. She was so bright, so articulate, so much more dainty than other girls. But that focus gradually shifted when it became clear Glinda was going to stand out in many more ways. She was so colorful, such a free spirit, so creative. Of course, all of those were code for "weird." Glinda was fine with that.

"So you maintain that you were not at Keesha Washington's house last night?" The younger detective flipped through his notebook. "I'm going to advise you to think about your answer. Lying could be considered obstructing justice."

The detectives somehow knew she was there. Keesha probably told them. She was probably annoyed that Glinda wasn't on her guest list but showed up anyway. Keesha would've explained that Glinda was breaking the law—the law of etiquette. Keesha had nearly jumped out of her skin when she stumbled upon Glinda the night before. She even called her a crazy bitch, though she said it more to herself than to Glinda. Keesha clearly was not comfortable with confrontation. Glinda almost felt sorry for her. Almost.

"Fine. I was there. But I wasn't at the party. I was near the party. It's more fun to watch."

"Where exactly were you?"

"I was hidden in some bushes. I know how that sounds, but it was quite comfortable. There was a wall and it was a good little spot. Kind of like when you're little and you make a blanket fort, you know?"

Blank stares. They apparently had never been children. Or never had blankets.

"I heard the whole argument between Mason and Kaylee. It was so hard to keep myself hidden. I wanted to jump up and yell, 'I told you so!' Like I said, I did tell him it would end badly. I just had no idea how badly." Once she got rolling, Glinda was perfectly happy to share what she knew with the detectives. She realized the more she talked, the longer she got to stay out of class.

"They were fighting outside the house, not far from where I was resting. Kaylee was screaming that she didn't cheat on him, but Mason kept saying that his 'dick said otherwise.'" Glinda thought that was high-larious, with a capital "high."

"What do you think he meant?"

"I don't want to be insulting here, but you really don't know? I get that you have to play the game a little, but really, you don't know what it means when someone says someone is cheating and the other person says his dick is talking to him?"

"So you think Kaylee gave Mason a venereal disease."

"I think Mason thought she did. Hey, you can find out with who if you just wait around and see who gets syphilis and goes blind! The red-tipped cane will be the crucial clue!" Glinda flashed to an image of blind students crowding the halls of Danbury, tripping over each other's canes.

"Tell us more about the argument. What exactly did they say?"

"Kaylee kept saying she wasn't cheating on Mason and that he didn't understand what had been happening." Mason and Glinda both, apparently. She had no idea what Kaylee was trying to say. The girl needed lessons in effective communication. "Kaylee screamed at Mason that he didn't understand, but then she didn't actually tell him anything to help him understand. She kept saying he didn't want to know the truth when clearly, that was the only thing he wanted. 'It can't be worse than what I'm thinking,' he'd told her." Glinda paused. "I don't want to go all Dr. Phil on you, but

I have to say that what Kaylee was really trying to say was that she didn't want to tell him the truth. Classic Psych 101. Projecting."

"So Mason was upset at this point?"

"Yes, Detective, he was upset. I mean, his dick was talking to him. That's upsetting. He screamed at Kaylee that he'd trusted her, and Kaylee yelled back she deserved his trust, which, of course, didn't make any sense if she had, in fact, given him some sort of infection. He told her he didn't want to see her again. Ever. He broke up with Kaylee. Right then. In front of everybody. No one was expecting that to happen. At least not this soon."

"How did Kaylee respond?"

"She was shocked. We all were. Then she got desperate. Mason turned to walk away, but she grabbed his arm. She was practically hanging on to him, trying to get him to stay. He shook her off. He started to storm off, but stopped when he realized Kaylee was on his heels. He saw her and was like, 'Don't look at me. Don't follow me. Don't come near me. If you follow me, I swear to God I'll kill you.'"

Glinda grinned at the detectives. Was that good or what?

13. BODY BAGS

"Have you tried the coffee house? Or the country club? I would help if I could, but I really don't know where they are."

Her phone vibrated as she got a text. Keesha held up a finger to keep the detectives from speaking. It was rude, but she was not at her best at the moment.

"Excuse me," she said, gesturing to her phone. "I need to read this." She looked down at the text message on her screen.

OMG. Coroner at K's. BODY BAGS.

Keesha's eyes flashed back to the detectives. "There's a coroner's truck at Kaylee's house? With body bags?" She struggled to keep her composure, but tears began to spill. "What's going on here? Who's dead? How many people are dead?"

"We're not at liberty to say," the older detective responded quietly.

"Are Kaylee and Mason dead? You need to tell me if my best friend is dead!"

The two detectives exchanged looks. She waited for them to respond, but they clearly had no intention of saying anything.

Keesha tried to control her breathing. She started to hear the familiar sound of her heartbeat in her ears. It happened whenever she got nervous. She knew she had to do something to calm herself or she would have a full-fledged panic attack. She took pains to stand up without rushing or seeming distressed. "If you'll excuse me."

She headed for the door. When the detectives moved to follow her, she put up a hand to stop them.

"I don't care if you're FBI or CIA or the Agents of SHIELD, you are not following me to the ladies' room."

Keesha strode out of the office and across the hall into the restroom. She went straight to the sinks and splashed water on her face, letting the information sink in. It seemed unreal. Body bags. Bags to put bodies in. There were dead bodies at Kaylee's house. Keesha refused to believe Kaylee was dead. She just could not handle the thought.

She dug around in her purse, searching. Finally, she pulled out what she wanted. No, what she needed. *Damn cap*, she thought, as she struggled to open the prescription bottle. Finally she twisted off the top and popped two of the little red pills, swallowing them dry.

She braced herself against the sink, staring at her tear-streaked reflection. She looked like a hag. She smoothed her hair and wiped the runny mascara from under her eyes. Better, but still not good enough. She closed her eyes and forced herself calm. Her shoulders back, her head held high, she opened her eyes and smiled at herself. Much better. That's the Keesha everybody knows.

⌇⌇⌇

"You need to tell us if Kaylee is one of the bodies."

Jared was equal parts livid and worried. These low-level grunts were refusing to give anyone information even though it had already spread through the school that Kaylee's house had become a crime scene complete with dead bodies and bloodstains. Yellow tape was draped across the Abernathy driveway and a coroner's van was waiting to be loaded. Did the police really think they could control the flow of information for long? Jared had already called his father to see what he could scare up. He, in turn, had put in calls to a friend from his squash league and another at the DA's office. It was only a matter of time before details of what was going on inside that house came out.

Jared thought back to the bruises on Kaylee's arm. When his attempt to get Mason expelled had failed, he'd gone to Kaylee's father to tell him what he had seen. The man was concerned, and grateful to Jared for coming forward. Jared knew he had eventually tried to get rid of Mason his own way, and that had failed as well. He wondered where Kaylee's father was now, if he was as sick as Jared was about the failure to get Mason under control before he did real harm.

"If Kaylee is dead, Mason killed her," Jared asserted to the police. "Why are you wasting time questioning their classmates when you should be out trying to find him? Do you realize how dangerous he is? For the safety of the students in this community, I demand to know what's going on."

Mason was wild. Jared was only starting to understand how wild. And now he was on the loose, and desperate. Who would he come for next?

"This just got so much more intriguing."

Glinda's BeDazzled phone was alight with messages about body bags, bloody clothing, and designer shoes. The shoe texts were standard because she subscribed to a bazillion fashion sites, but body bags and anything bloody were way out of the norm. The only thing that would be more interesting to her was if someone had been beaten to a bloody pulp with a pair of designer heels. But alas, she didn't think that was the case here.

She looked up at the detectives hoping to get a reaction that would reveal something she could post online. They were stone-faced.

"I heard it was murder-suicide." They also seemed to be watching her closely. "I guess that makes a lot more sense than suicide-murder. I mean you couldn't kill yourself and then kill someone else." She smiled, hoping for any hint as to what was happening. "I heard there were two bodies but three body bags because they were cut up in little pieces."

She scanned their faces for a clue. They weren't obliging. This was going to be tougher than she thought.

———

"I heard that her entire family was killed except Anne." Trevor shuddered. "Oh my God. Does Anne know? Has anybody told her? This is going to destroy her."

"So the family was close?" The younger detective smiled at Trevor. He had remarkably good teeth for a cop. At least, for what Trevor thought a cop would look like up close.

"Do you have to be close to be upset your family was slaughtered? I mean, I have my own mommy and daddy issues and I'd still be a little disturbed if they ended up in garbage bags."

"Did they all get along?"

"So they did end up in garbage bags?" He felt himself fighting the urge to vomit.

"We did not say that."

"You didn't deny it."

"We're not here to give you information." The older detective seemed annoyed, but the younger one was taking a softer approach. "There were no garbage bags involved. You were about to tell us if they all got along."

"I don't know. They took vacations together and looked really good in pictures. Her parents tolerated each other and drank a lot. Just like my parents and the parents of every other student in this school."

"Do you think they were happy?"

"Define 'happy.'" Trevor was fast losing respect for the legal establishment and the cute detective in particular. "That's harder to do than defining if a family was 'close.' Do you understand the questions you're asking can have a million different answers?" It occurred to him that that might be their tactic—asking impossible questions to let their interrogation subjects fill in whatever blanks they thought were relevant. It was a game and while he ordinarily would enjoy such verbal ping-pong, Trevor was in no mood at the moment.

"You have to tell me what happened. I can't keep dancing around my words, not knowing if I'm talking about somebody who's alive or dead. Do you know how cruel this is? Kaylee is my friend. Was my friend. You know what? Screw you. I don't have to answer any questions."

He stared at the detectives, daring them to say something. But they used the silence and waited. Trevor tried to hold his own silence, but he knew he couldn't. Kaylee always called him a megamouth. When they were small they would hold contests to see who could be quiet the longest. Kaylee won every time. He couldn't handle the thought of losing her. He had to help the detectives find her. If she was mad at him for giving information to them he'd deal with it. If she was mad at him that meant she was alive.

"What exactly do you want to know that will help you find her?"

14. TAKING THE EDGE OFF

"I don't care what anybody heard Mason say. I don't believe he would hurt Kaylee."

Keesha was back facing the detectives, her hair and make-up perfect. The pills she'd taken went a long way to helping regain her composure.

"Did you hear the argument?" The younger detective asked. Keesha couldn't be sure, but she thought he was looking at her a little too closely. Maybe he suspected she was on something. Keesha had heard police officers could tell. She sat up even straighter and smiled at them both.

"I was too busy overseeing the party last night and I didn't hear them."

Of course, that was only partly true. Keesha did take her host-essing duties seriously. She wanted everyone to have a good time, but she didn't want them to destroy anything. Her father adored his mahogany bar in their den. He babied it, oiling it and fretting over every little nick. Keesha knew that one errant beer bottle would leave a ring. So she provided coasters, but that didn't always work. People were careless. She had to keep an eye on things.

She did take a little break at one point during the night, but she would never tell the detectives about it. She was waiting outside the house for Ernie to arrive. Ernie was another tutor she'd met while volunteering for a literacy program downtown. When she mentioned how tense she was, he offered her a little something to take the edge off. She wished she could say she was naive and he tricked her, but she knew exactly what he was offering and she took it. She actually delighted a bit in how wicked it seemed. No one would ever expect that Keesha Washington, president of the debate society, the service club, and student United Nations, was an addict. When she won the Volunteer of the Year award that year, Ernie was in the front of the crowd, cheering the loudest along with her parents. It made her a little sick and a little excited to know that all he had to do was turn and tell them the truth about their relationship and her entire world would collapse.

And the thing was, the drugs worked a little too well. Keesha was using more to keep the same even keel. The night of the party, she found herself waiting near the end of her driveway for Ernie to make another delivery when Mason and Kaylee were having their now epic argument. If she didn't have her own agenda, she would've gone to check it out. But she needed to see Ernie and was afraid if she wandered off, he would come looking for her, or worse, leave without making the delivery.

She always had such mixed feelings when she saw Ernie. He brought her relief, pure and simple, but also shame. She knew her parents would be disappointed if they knew and would probably blame themselves for some imagined parenting failure. They would whisk her off to the best rehab money could buy and would make her switch to a less stressful school to prevent a relapse. The thing was, they were great parents. They loved her and supported her. Whatever hell Keesha faced, she brought on herself. That was why she was so upset when she found out Jared had a recording of her popping pills. She could handle the gossip from her peers, she told herself. They might not even believe it because she had such a reputation for being very much on top of things.

But it would crush her parents if they found out. That, she couldn't handle. She'd had no choice but to back out of the election. When she told her parents about the decision, they hugged her and said they'd support whatever she did. That was so them. It was like their unconditional love was a pressure all its own.

When Ernie arrived last night, they made the exchange quickly. Ernie wanted to join the party, but she would never allow that to happen. While his wares would undoubtedly be welcomed, Keesha wasn't ready to let her two worlds collide like that. He tried to walk past her to go inside, but she held her arm out to block him from entering. She could tell she'd hurt his feelings. He thought of himself as her friend. He was, in a way, as much as an addict was friends with a dealer. Really, he was the only person who knew her darkest secret.

The older detective interrupted her thoughts. "Tell us what you remember."

"I was outside picking up some empties when I heard the bushes rustling." Keesha didn't mention that she'd immediately assumed Jared was spying on her again. "I thought it might be two people making out, but when I got close, my classmate Glinda jumped out and started running. She nearly knocked me over." Glinda was wearing heels that had to be at least seven inches tall. Seven-inch heels to hide in the bushes and spy on people. Crazy bitch. Keesha watched the little waif run off into the night.

"When I turned to go back to the house, Mason rushed by. He nearly knocked the empties out of my hand," The truth was he nearly knocked the pill bottle out of her hand, but, of course, she wouldn't say that to the police. Mason blew by her and didn't look back, even when she yelled, in her angriest voice, "*Excuse me!*" That was as close as she ever got to fighting words.

She totally missed what got him so upset, but could tell something major was going on. If she'd known it had anything to do with Kaylee, of course she would've sought her out and offered to help.

Mason and Kaylee were from opposite ends of the universe, and it still somehow worked. But now something had happened and she was doubting her assessment of Mason. He was rough around the edges. She knew that. Everybody did. He never hid who he was.

"So you did see that Mason was upset about something before he left," the older detective prodded.

"He was upset," Keesha said. "But who wouldn't be upset when they just broke up with the love of their life?"

"We've heard he was known for being violent."

Keesha shook her head. "He was not typical, and it made people uncomfortable."

"Explain."

"He knew how to fix stuff and got animated when he got upset. But he also helped his father around the grounds, even though other students would see him. He didn't care what they thought. *That* made them uncomfortable. It's part of what I liked about him."

15.CHARITY CASE

"All I know is that if it's my boy they found in that garage and you're sitting here asking me about what I knew about who in this wannabe prep school instead of letting me go see him, you're going to have to deal with me later."

Mike Henry fumed. He'd heard the rumors that Mason had killed the Abernathy girl and run away. He knew his boy would never do that. He loved the girl, or thought he did. Mason had a temper and had been in a few scrapes in the past, but would never lay a hand on a woman. Mike had drilled that into his head.

So if Mason hadn't killed her, it stood to reason that his might be one of the bodies they found. Mike had to believe the cops would have told him by now. He would *not* let himself get emotional.

This mess was all his fault. He'd known Mason was way smarter than he himself ever was and had a chance to be whatever he wanted. He'd taken the job at Danbury so Mason could get the best education possible. Mike grew up one town over and had known without a doubt that he would always be one of the workers and the kids who went to Danbury would always be the bosses. When the job came open, Mike bristled at taking it and fulfilling his own depressing prediction, until he found out that it entailed free tuition for his kid. Everything fell into place. His son would go on scholarship to a school whose tuition was more than Mike made in a year. A school where no one thought he would do well.

"We understand Mason has made some waves in his time here," the younger detective said. Mike wondered if "made some waves" was the new way of saying "pissed people off."

"People didn't think he belonged here, that he was some charity case," Mike kept his voice steady. "That he was less than, because he was my son."

But Mason proved he belonged there, in class anyway. He aced his tests but still fought the prejudices that came with being working class. These people, the ones who would never admit thinking less of anyone because of their race or religion, openly judged people who worked with their hands and made an honest wage.

And Mike had planted his son square in the middle of them all. It was important to Mike that these detectives understood what Mason was up against. They were judging him without understanding how prejudiced people were. "When my son got a perfect score on a test, his teachers assumed he cheated. The dean assumed he cheated. Other students assumed he cheated.

Their small little minds couldn't fathom that he was just that smart and worked that hard."

Mike told the detectives about seeing the connection for the first time between Mason and the Abernathy girl. "Me and Mason were working outside in the flower beds in front of the school. I didn't like him to work like that where his classmates could see him, but he insisted on helping. That's the kind of kid my son is."

The detectives nodded like they agreed with his assessment, but Mike knew they would nod at anything he said to get him to keep talking.

"When Kaylee walked by with some of her uptight friends, Mason practically tripped over himself to talk to her. She was cute, I'll give her that. But I warned him about her family."

"You have a history with the Abernathys?"

"History is a strong word. But yeah, years back, my sister, Jolene, was a housekeeper for them. She'd come home with tales of shenanigans that seemed better suited to a soap opera than a real-life family." They looked good and made it a point to contribute to the town, but Mike and his family knew the Abernathys were morally bankrupt. They paid her well, but in the end, the cost was great. Mike didn't care how sweet Kaylee seemed. He knew she was an Abernathy. "The whole lot of them is trouble."

"We understand her father didn't want the two of them to date either."

"He thought his little girl was too good for my son. He wanted me to keep Mason away from Kaylee."

"And what did you do?"

"I told him to shove it up his waxed and bleached asshole, and that if I heard him bring that up again, I'd demonstrate what I meant." Mike smirked at the memory. William Abernathy IV was surprised at his reaction. William the Fourth. Who the hell did these people think they were, British royalty? His wife had always joked about "the Romans," people who had Roman numerals after their names. Marianne said they represented what fraction of sanity they had left. So the farther down the family line you got, the less sane people were. Henry VIII was a perfect example of a nut job, she'd say. She always made Mike laugh. Mason got his smarts from her.

"What did Mr. Abernathy do when you threatened him?"

"Threaten is a strong word. I told him I wasn't going to listen to him, and that my son was too good for his daughter."

"How did he react?"

"He threatened to get me fired if they stayed together."

"That must have made you angry."

"No, it made me happy," he said sarcastically. "Of course

it made me angry. He told me he'd get me fired and I got angry. Why do you care so much about my fight with him?"

The older detective had no intention of answering the question. "What did you do when he threatened to get you fired?"

"I told him the truth—that getting me fired would have the opposite effect of what he wanted. I told him it would keep his little girl going back to my Mason for months, even years. Maybe he'd end up as his son-in-law. Asshole thinks he's so smart, but what he didn't seem to understand is that getting me fired would just give Mason and Kaylee a common enemy—him. Nothing brings two people together like hating the same thing."

"So you supported their relationship?"

"I didn't say that. I warned Mason off of the girl. I know that family. Like I said, my sister, Mason's aunt, used to work for them years ago. They're trouble."

"Trouble how?"

"Are you listening to me? They're trouble the way rich, arrogant assholes always are. They don't care what they do to other people."

"So Kaylee was like that?"

"Stop putting words in my mouth. Kaylee seemed like a nice kid, her sister too. God knows how, coming from those two. I've been around rich assholes a long time, detective. I know that nothing good comes of normal people mixing it up with them."

"So you didn't have a thing against Kaylee, you just knew Mason should stay away from that family?"

"Correct. And I was right."

"How so?"

He gestured to the surrounding room and the detectives, his voice ominous. "I warned him that the Abernathys are nothing but trouble. And look what's going on. I'd call this trouble."

16.MENIAL TASK

Olivia firmly pressed the stick into the mound of sheets in the trunk of her husband's Mercedes. A red spot appeared, flowering as the wetness spread into a large crimson stain.

Taking another breath, she pulled back the covers to see whom William had killed.

His lifeless eyes stared back up.

Even in death, he was beautiful. Such cheekbones.

Olivia shook her head and exhaled. She was relieved. She wasn't sure who she would find when she pulled back the bloody covers. Some small part of her had worried it was Kaylee. Or even Mason. William certainly hated Mason. He'd ranted about him when he discovered Kaylee was dating him. He felt certain Kaylee was doing it only to rebel, not because of any real feelings for him. The boy knew exactly how to push his buttons. She wondered if he'd pushed too far and they fought. Mason was strong enough to over-power William. She couldn't tell how he had died, except that it was clearly bloody. What a horrible way to end up, wrapped like a cigar in the trunk of a car. Olivia hadn't loved William for years, but she would not have wished this end for him. She wondered who would.

Mason would definitely be a suspect. Even Kaylee, probably, and who knows what other enemies William had made. He was the picture of an upstanding Danbury citizen, but Olivia knew he had pissed off a lot of people. He was very competitive and viewed business as a game to be won.

Some people might consider Olivia a suspect. Her lover too.

With that thought in mind, Olivia eyed the bloodstains around the edge of the trunk. She felt a catch in her throat. These sloppy red smears had come from her husband's dead body. The culprit probably left fingerprints that would lead police right to him. Or her. She thought of Kaylee. She didn't think her daughter capable of such violence, but she was young and in love, people were known to do profoundly stupid things in that state.

Olivia decided to make the police's job a little more difficult.

She slipped off her bloody shoes and made her way back to the kitchen, where she filled a bucket with hot, sudsy water. The sun played off the bubbles as it filled. It was quite pretty, really.

She pulled on some yellow rubber gloves, the kind she used to wear to wash dishes back when she did menial tasks, and headed back to the garage. She got to work cleaning around the trunk and wiping whatever surface might hold the killer's fingerprints. It was soothing to have a simple task to do.

She thought back to the early days with William. At first, she'd been swept away by how big his world seemed. His family had money for so long they'd forgotten exactly where it came from. That's what it seemed at the time, anyway. Eventually she learned that not all of their business dealings were legitimate, so the family found it best not to talk about them. But they enjoyed the spoils. They ate at the finest restaurants, traveled the world, and never once fretted over a bill.

Olivia had been raised comfortably. Her father was a lawyer and she never wanted for anything. She went to the finest schools and traveled abroad with her parents every summer, but the Abernathys took living well to an entirely different level. They found it quaint when she taught William how to cook an egg and when his mother learned she occasionally did her own nails. The regal woman didn't even know a person could buy nail polish remover at the drugstore. She'd never picked up a prescription or ran to the store to buy milk. They had people who did that. The thing that had surprised Olivia was how gracious her mother-in-law was. She had been groomed to entertain and delight, and she did until she died, her hair carefully coiffed and her silk peignoir arranged perfectly.

Olivia realized now that marrying into the family had its price, but she wasn't sure if she had to do it over again, what she would do. She might have achieved her dream of being a grand ballerina, or she might not have made the cut and ended up an ordinary housewife someplace far less fabulous. She and her husband had not been a true team for years, but she had to admit that because of him, her life had been a fun ride mostly. She looked into the trunk at William's blank eyes. He might have done things differently if he had had the chance.

She put away the cleaning evidence and picked up her phone. She dialed and listened to it ring on the other end until someone picked up. "Nine-one-one. How can I help you?"

Olivia took a few quick breaths, trying not to sound overly calm.

"Operator, I would like to report that someone has murdered my husband."

17. THE BACK OF THE PATROL CAR

The fourteen-year-old girl with long brown hair sat on the sofa next to her mother in the family's comfortably modern living room. Her almond-shaped eyes were red from crying. Her father was dead and the police suspected her sister and her boyfriend of killing him. Anne couldn't really process all of it.

She'd started the day like every other one. That was what struck her now. She woke up. Got showered and dressed. Left for school, waving at her mom before she got in the minivan with her neighbor. She'd heard that Kaylee and Mason had ditched for the day, and so she texted her sister, but didn't think much when she didn't get a response. If Kaylee was ditching with Mason, she was hardly going to be checking her phone that much.

Then History class. They were learning about the Great Depression, but Anne was daydreaming. She liked to think about the 1920s and the elegant clothes and the jazz music. Mr. Mockus came up to her. She thought she was in trouble for not paying attention.

"Miss Abernathy?"

"I'm sorry. I was up late last night. I didn't mean to zone out. Let me find the page." Anne started to flip through her text, but the teacher put a gentle hand on her shoulder. "Please gather your things and step outside."

The guidance counselor, Mrs. Wood, was waiting for her. Anne knew that was a bad sign.

"Something has happened," she said. She reached out and put her hand on Anne's shoulder, like she was following a grief-counseling script.

"What do you mean? Is it Kaylee?"

"No, dear. It's your father."

"What about him?"

"Something has happened to him. You need to go with the police." When Anne didn't move, the counselor gave her a gentle nudge in the direction of the school's ornate formal entrance hall.

Anne didn't really understand what she was saying. *"Something has happened to your father. . . . The police."* She had the distinct sense her life would never be the same.

She waited at the main entrance to the school and when the police car pulled up, everything around her shifted. She could see the strobing lights, but couldn't hear anything. Not the wind rustling in the trees, or the sound trucks passing on the road nearby. Anne walked toward the car and stood next to the back door.

"Miss, you can sit in the front with me, unless you're more comfortable in back." The uniformed police officer also spoke gently to her, gesturing to the open passenger-side door. She felt a little foolish. Of course she would sit in front. No one was accusing her of anything.

They rode in silence, the occasional static from his radio scratching the air. She didn't have to tell him which house was hers. He pulled up the driveway and gave her a sympathetic smile before she got out. "You take care of yourself, Miss."

"I will. Thank you."

She got out and took a deep breath. Signs of the police were everywhere outside the modern stone-and-glass home. Cruisers dotted the street. Crime scene tape was draped across the garage.

Anne's mother was waiting near the door while several police officers were milling about inside. Olivia held out her arms to hug her daughter when she entered, but Anne just breezed by. Her mother never hugged her. She wasn't going to let her start now.

She barely had time to put her backpack down and drink some water when a tall female detective approached. "We'd like to ask you some questions now."

"Of course." Anne was still stunned. Her father was dead. Kaylee and Mason were missing. And she was being questioned by the police. Her mother did most of the answering as a male detective took notes. He was clearly following the lead of the female and barely spoke.

"Where was Mr. Abernathy last night?"

"I'm not entirely sure. I didn't see him before dinner."

"We understand he wasn't fond of your daughter's boyfriend."

"He wasn't fond of anyone she dated."

"It had nothing to do with Mason's temper?"

"Not that I know of."

It all sounded so wrong to Anne. She thought about why they were asking so many questions about Mason and Kaylee. They thought they had something to do with her father's murder. This was unacceptable. She wanted to make sure the police weren't wasting time with crazy theories. Her father might be dead, but Kaylee was alive. The police needed to make sure she got home safely. "Mason isn't violent. Kaylee wouldn't be with somebody violent."

Anne also knew Mason and Kaylee didn't kill her father. She knew it just like she knew she was right-handed. Mason and Kaylee were a perfect couple, not violent outlaws.

"What if they were witnesses to the murder and they're scared because the killer knows they saw him?" The detectives smiled politely.

"You think they're on the run to hide from the perpetrator?" The female detective asked, her voice dripping disbelief. "If they were frightened, wouldn't they come to the police?"

"I don't know what they would do if they'd witnessed a murder." Anne shook her head as she spoke. "But you need to be looking for them to make sure they're safe, not because they're suspects. If police think they're suspects, they could end up shot or something."

"You're close with your sister?"

"Yes, of course we got along. What does that have to do with anything?"

"My daughters never fought. They were so close it was enviable." For once, her mother added something useful.

Anne and Kaylee had always been close even though they were like opposite sides of a coin, maybe because they *were* opposites. Where Kaylee was outgoing, Anne was shy. Anne was a good student but Kaylee wasn't concerned with grades. They never competed for the same things. They got attention in their own ways, though mostly it was Kaylee who got the attention. Anne was fine with that. Kaylee would try to draw Anne into the spotlight with her, telling her little sister that she was beautiful and fabulous, but Anne wasn't interested. She'd tolerated when Kaylee showed her how to apply makeup to her light blue eyes to best show them off, or showed her how to do her hair, but it was mostly because she enjoyed spending time with her sister. Anne would have been just as happy listening to music or reading or watching TV together.

"Anne, did you see Kaylee or Mason last night?"

"I sat in Kaylee's room as she got ready for Keesha's party."

"Did anything seem unusual to you?"

"She was fine. She tried on ten dresses and then after she picked one, she tried on ten different pairs of shoes to go with it."

That was all typical Kaylee. "Kaylee waited for Mason to pick her up but he never showed. That was really unusual. Kaylee was worried about him. She thought he might have crashed his new car."

"He has a new car?" The male detective wrote this down. "Is he a safe driver?"

"I wouldn't let my daughter go around with someone who wasn't," Olivia said.

"He drives fast, but I was never scared when I was in the car with him." Anne thought back to the night before, wondering if Kaylee had given off any clues about what would happen. "I don't think Kaylee even realized Mason was mad about something. She was more concerned." Even Anne was worried. She told Kaylee to let her know what had happened to him.

She never did. Anne eventually figured things were fine and went to bed. Kaylee would fill her in on the details later. But, of course, she never did. Anne had no idea what had prompted her sister to run away last night. She felt certain that if the cops just found Kaylee, she would be able to clear up the entire mess and prove her innocence.

"Where do you think she might go, if she did run away?"

"Kaylee likes Indian things. Native American. Like beads and stuff. If she were going somewhere, I think she'd go someplace like Arizona, or New Mexico."

The male detective wrote this down in his notebook.

"She has a trust fund. Money she can use if she has to."

"Do you think Kaylee would give money to Mason?"

"He's not like that. You want to paint Mason like he's some dirtball but you're not actually listening to what I'm saying. Mason would not make Kaylee do anything she didn't want to do. He just wouldn't. He's a gentleman."

Olivia Abernathy sat silently during much of the police's questioning of Anne, but she couldn't maintain her calm any longer. She turned to her daughter. "I don't know why you've created this image of Mason that's nothing like reality. He's not some working-class hero. He's a smart boy who has shown on more than one occasion to have a bad temper and even worse judgment."

Anne shook her head, but Olivia continued.

"Rough hands are just that. Rough."

Lily Mars had been crying. She'd never known anybody who had died before, let alone been murdered. Her attitude was more subdued than before.

"How was he killed?" she asked hesitantly. It seemed like an important question.

Rumors were flying around the school. Her phone was flashing with texts about it. According to her classmates, William Abernathy had been stabbed, shot, choked, clubbed, burned, suffocated, poisoned, gored, or decapitated. In other words, no one had any idea what happened to him.

The only thing people seemed to agree on was that it was violent. It was not a cool and calculated crime. William had suffered. Someone really hated him. She almost smiled at how stupid that thought was. People don't kill people they love.

"Did he have any enemies you knew of," the younger detective asked.

"He was found dead in a trunk, right?" She raised her eyebrows. "I'm pretty sure that means he had at least one enemy." She couldn't be of much help in that department. "Talk to Mason's father, Mike

Henry. They'd had an argument not too long ago."

"What was it about?"

"Ask him. I have no idea. One thing you have to understand, Detectives, is that the help yield a significant amount of power in our world."

"How's that?"

"They can be standing in a room and no one sees them, so they're frequently witnesses to the worst behaviors of their employers. They know things," she explained. "Things people don't want other people to know."

What did Mike Henry know?

"Yes, I fought with the deceased, but no, I did not kill the man." Mike Henry felt an incredible sense of relief when he heard William Abernathy's was the only body police found at the house. He'd been worried about his son and hoped to God the boy had nothing to do with the death. But for now, he was just grateful Mason was alive. He smiled at the cops. "Twenty guys at Kelly's bar will tell you where I was last night." Twenty was an exaggeration. Twenty were there, to be sure, but they were drinking heavily and only ten guys would actually be able to remember the evening.

"Mr. Abernathy is *dead*?" Jared digested this. He was shocked, and sad, but at the same time it must mean Kaylee was alive. At least for now. The police confirmed there was only one body in the trunk of the car. "If Kaylee and Mason are missing, you need to assume he killed her father and forced her to leave with him. There's no way Kaylee would have anything to do with this. She would never leave with Mason if he did that. Never."

Jared thought about the Abernathys. He'd heard the police had pulled Anne out of History class earlier in the morning, right before word broke about the body bags. Rumor had it she had to identify whatever bodies were found. Jared hoped that wasn't true. That was an adult's job. Jared wondered what made Mason kill Abernathy then and not earlier when they'd confronted one another. Abernathy knew Mason was a bad influence on his daughter. When Jared found the bruises on Kaylee, he'd told her father about them. Jared thought that was probably the tipping point, the incident that made him try to break them up. Mason had somehow gotten out of that too.

Kaylee's father had been pleased when Jared had asked his daughter out. They'd known each other in some capacity for years through the Country Club. Most of the families at Danbury belonged. Kids learned to golf and play tennis as soon as they learned to walk. William Abernathy had taken Jared golfing as soon as he found out he was dating Kaylee. He was warm and encouraging and wanted to know all about Jared's plans for the future. Jared could see where Kaylee got her good nature. Mr. Abernathy knew how to listen and how to make a person feel important. And his golf game was outstanding.

Jared's father said he was known for being a shark in the business world, that he could smell his opponents' weaknesses. Yet Jared saw him with his daughters at various social events and the man was nothing but gentle. He had even been named the Danbury City Community Leader last year for his work in bringing a factory to town that provided more than a hundred jobs. Certainly Abernathy Holdings would benefit, but so would all those workers.

"Tell us about the relationship between Mason and William Abernathy."

"He didn't want Kaylee dating Mason. And not because he was the son of a laborer. He didn't want his daughter dating him because he was volatile and rebellious in the worst way. He rebelled against nothing and everything. He had a chance at a good education and he was pissing off the people who provided it every chance he got. What father would want his little girl going out with someone like that?"

"Did he actually take any sort of action against Mason?"

"I heard there was something," Jared informed them. "With money involved. Lots of it." Abernathy had sensed Mason's weakness and wanted to capitalize on it. He was, indeed, a shark.

19.YOU PEOPLE HAVE SAFES, DON'T YOU?

Kaylee was home early from school and had been enjoying the quiet of the house when she heard familiar voices in the living room. Mason was talking with her father? It was more than unusual; it was unbelievable. Her father had basically declared war on Mason, yet here he was. She crept close and stood silently in the hallway.

Mason sat across from her father, the tastefully modern coffee table between them. Mason's leather jacket contrasting with the socialite's Oxford shirt and cashmere sweater. Mason hadn't been sure what to expect when Abernathy called and invited him to the house. For a brief moment, he thought he might actually be trying to get to know him. Mason smiled. Kaylee's innocence had been rubbing off on him. But then the prick spoke. "You need to break up with my daughter." Mason immediately stood up and turned toward the door.

"Sit," Abernathy commanded.

"Screw you. I'm not a dog."

Kaylee smiled. She knew Mason would stand up to him.

"Sit. You'll want to hear my offer." To Kaylee's dismay, Mason sat. He wasn't supposed to entertain anything resembling an offer about breaking up with her.

"So there's an offer?" Mason was suspicious.

Abernathy pulled a pile of cash out from a shelf under the table and put it between them. He kept his eyes on Mason as he slid the money toward him. "You are going to break up with Kaylee."

Mason picked up the cash and carefully counted it—one hundred fifty-dollar bills in all. "Five thousand dollars?"

Kaylee cringed. This was no small gesture. That was big money to anyone, let alone someone like Mason. She felt her body tightening, waiting for his response. He had to reject it. He had to. He loved her.

"You think I'll break up with your daughter for five thousand dollars?" Kaylee felt herself relax. Mason was about to get going and tell her father what he could do with his money. But instead, he shook his head. "This isn't enough." She heard him drop the money on the table. Kaylee fought the urge to scream out.

"What?" Abernathy had expected the punk to protest before taking the payment just to save face, but he did not expect him to bargain.

"Double it and we'll talk."

"My offer is on the table."

"You want me to consider it, stop insulting me. Go get your checkbook or go to your safe. You people have safes, don't you? And get more money." He pushed the cash back toward him. "You probably spend this much eating out in a month. I want real bones."

Kaylee couldn't listen anymore. She thought of the times she had defended Mason, had defended his honor and decency to people. She'd been wrong about everything. With that thought, she slipped away toward the back door of the house, already dialing her phone. In between sobs, she told Trevor she was going to the park where they used to play as kids. She knew he'd drop what he was doing to be with her.

In the living room, Abernathy considered Mason before quietly rising to do as he asked. Once alone, Mason looked around. Everything was beautifully decorated. It was modern, but somewhat warm. A wall of glass looked out on the pool. A party house. Mason wondered why Kaylee never had any. When Abernathy returned, the cash pile was twice as big.

He handed it to Mason, his voice authoritative. "Of course you won't mention this when you break up with her."

"Don't worry. She'll only hate one of us."

This seemed to be the final insult. Abernathy nearly spat his words. "You're just a blip in her life. A momentary diversion that she might mention some day when she talks about boys she dated in high school. I'm her father."

Mason grinned at the irony. "Right. Her image of a good man." His blood was boiling. He never felt more sorry for Kaylee, to have this asshole raise her. She'd been given every advantage in life, except a decent father. What a role model. Mason mentally thanked his own dad. He may have been uneducated and downright gruff, but he was a good man. "Here's the thing . . ."

"We're done here." Abernathy was accustomed to calling the shots, but Mason wasn't accustomed to listening to anyone.

"Here's the thing. I'm not breaking up with Kaylee."

"Maybe I wasn't clear. You're breaking up with her. One way or another, I will make it happen. I didn't have to offer you anything."

"Add *generous* to all those great things people think about you." Mason shook his head.

"If I see you with Kaylee, hear about you with Kaylee, anything. I will call the police and say you stole that money."

"No. You won't."

"You little self-righteous shit. You seem to be mistaking me for some powerless sap like your father."

Mason nearly hit him then. He made a fist but fought the urge. This had to end with him in control. "You won't report me, because if you do, to anyone, I'll tell them what I know."

"Make up any story you want. No one will believe you." But the man clearly was uncomfortable. Mason let the silence sit. The prick probably had several big secrets and wasn't sure which one he was talking about. But Mason knew the one he had was a game changer. Screw this asshole for thinking he wasn't good enough for his daughter. Screw him for thinking he could be bought like a whore. Screw him for underestimating Mason Henry.

20.STALKARAZZI

"It's sort of unethical, really, if you think about it," Glinda reasoned. Kaylee's dad offered money to Mason to break up with his daughter, and Mason took the money but refused to hold up his end of the bargain. "If I gave money to someone to buy a really great fringed leather jacket, and they took the money but gave me a jacket that didn't have fringe, I'd be hellza angry. And this is way worse. I mean, he didn't even get the jacket. Forget the fringe." Glinda was sure William Abernathy must have felt the same way. "Do you think this might be what led to his getting killed? Like, the old man went after Mason and they fought?"

"So people at school knew what happened with her father?" The old detective sounded impatient.

"Of course. Word got out. And it was obvious when Kaylee started avoiding Mason."

"They were still together as of last night."

"But they almost broke up before over it. I saw the whole thing. I was on a balcony at school." Again, very Ruliet.

"So they fought. . . ." The older detective was also tired.

"Right. Mason was sitting on the steps after school. He was

throwing rocks at a fire hydrant, looking all angsty. I waited around to see what was going on. He has a total crap arm, by the way. Couldn't hit the hydrant to save his life."

"Go on."

"What else can I say about it? He wasn't a jock."

"Go on about the fight."

"At this point, everybody knew something was up with the two of them. Kaylee had missed a few days of school, and when she came back, she was always getting to class late or leaving early. Totally not like her. Word on the street was she was doing that so Mason never had a chance to be alone with her and to talk to her. Apparently, he was getting tired of trying to track her down, so here he was, sitting and waiting like a stalkarazzi for her to walk by. When Kaylee came out of the building and saw him waiting, she was all ready to turn around, but for whatever reason, she didn't. She walked down the steps, right by him, and he called out to her. He asked why she hadn't answered any of his calls or texts. Kaylee had to hear him, but she pretended she didn't. Then he chased after her. He said he wanted to show her something." Glinda paused. "That really got my interest."

～～

Kaylee had been avoiding Mason after the incident between him and her father. The last thing she'd heard was Mason taking the money to break up with her. She was furious and heartbroken. She almost turned around when she saw him waiting for her outside of school, but she wanted to have the fight and just get it over with.

Still, she didn't approach him and made him chase after her. "Why are you avoiding me?"

"Why would I want to meet with you when I know it's so you can break up with me?" It seemed like a good question to her, but Mason seemed genuinely confused.

"What are you talking about? I'm not breaking up with you. Ever."

Kaylee finally stopped to face him. "I really thought we had something. Something more than all this." She gestured to the school and the few students nearby.

"We do. You know I'd do anything for you. Anything." His eyes pleaded with hers.

"You're lying. I know about the money. I saw you with my father. I know you cut a deal." Mason finally understood why she'd been avoiding him. What a mess.

"Please, let me explain."

"There's no explaining what you did. I thought I meant

something more to you. I thought you knew that money couldn't buy what we had."

"Money can't buy what we have. Nothing can. People could spend their whole lives searching and never have what we have."

The more Mason protested, the more upset Kaylee got. She never believed he could be such a hypocrite. "I trusted you."

"I deserve your trust! I would do anything for you. I know I'm lucky to have you."

"You're lying."

"I'm not. I won't. I will never do anything to hurt you."

Kaylee couldn't even look at him. She knew if she did she'd burst into tears. She tried to escape before she lost it, looking down so he wouldn't see her eyes, but Mason grabbed her. "Look at me. Yes. I took the money." Kaylee yanked away, but Mason wasn't letting go. "But I'm not breaking up with you."

"*You took my father's money,*" Kaylee spat out the words.

"I did. I took his money. He offered me money to break up with you, and I took it. But I'm not breaking up with you. I never planned to break up with you. Ever. If you'll have me, you'll be stuck with me forever."

Now it was Kaylee's turn to be confused. Mason shook his head. "I can't be bought. Not by him or anybody else."

"But he paid you."

"He did. But he's a fool who thinks he can fix problems by throwing cash at them. He offered money and I took it." When Mason recounted this part, he seemed pleased with himself, like he'd outsmarted someone who was trying to trick him. But Kaylee knew her father better than Mason did. He wouldn't give up that easily. She didn't like what her father did trying to buy Mason out, and she was secretly relieved that Mason wasn't breaking up with her, but his double crossing her father worried her.

"My father isn't going to just walk away. You took his money. He'll make things hard on you. Maybe on your father. You need to think about what you're doing."

"He won't do anything."

"You don't know him the way I do."

"I know something. Something he doesn't want anybody else to know." Mason held her gaze. He thought she would be pleased he had bested her father. He expected her to ask what the information was, but instead Kaylee looked concerned.

"This thing you know. Does it have something to do with me?"

Mason smiled. "You don't have any secrets this big."

Kaylee wished he was right.

"I need to show you something."

Mason took Kaylee's hand and guided her around the corner

of the building to where a dark gray Mustang was parked. It was a muscle car, all waxed and sexy.

"What's this?"

"It's the car your father bought us. You don't have to ride around in my old piece of shit anymore."

"What are you talking about?"

"Your father gave me the money. I bought a car. It's simple."

"My father must be furious," Kaylee said. Mason hugged her. "Let him be furious," he said. "He can't hurt us."

Kaylee looked doubtful. If she'd looked up toward the balcony, she would've seen that Glinda looked doubtful as well. Mason was screwing with some powerful people.

"Mr. Abernathy offered Mason money to break up with Kaylee. Mason took the money and bought that white-trash hot rod of his. That's how little he thinks of Kaylee. Everybody thinks he loved her so much. But he was willing to be bought off."

Jared was getting impatient. He didn't see why the police needed to rehash all this information when they should be out looking for Mason and Kaylee.

"And then he didn't break up with her," Jared pointed out. "He made a deal and didn't honor it. That was Mason, no sense of decency."

"Why didn't Abernathy report the incident? Mason had essentially stolen money from him."

"Rumor had it that Mason knew something about the man and was blackmailing him. What he knew, I have no idea." Jared realized he needed to find out. There was a lot going on with Mason that he didn't know about. First, he managed to avoid getting punished for throwing Jared into the lockers. Then, he took a large amount of money from William Abernathy without honoring the agreement they had, and Abernathy had let him go unscathed. Mason clearly knew something, something that the people who ordinarily would be able to punish him wanted kept secret. Jared couldn't tolerate the thought of Mason being better at the information game than he was.

He left the interrogation and immediately pulled up his computer with recordings from the various camera feeds he had around the campus. He settled into a comfortable chair in the student lounge. There was a lot of footage to sort through and Jared wasn't sure where to start. He knew it had something to do with William Abernathy, so he pulled footage from the day he received his community service award. Most of his cameras and bugs were in places people had private conversations: locker rooms, restrooms, the dean's office. Jared was surprised at how many people popped pills, or worse, in public restrooms. They seemed so dirty for something so personal. Maybe Mr. Abernathy had a drug problem. That seemed the most likely.

Jared thought of his sizable trove of information. He knew things about numerous students and he was waiting until he needed to use them. He'd known about Keesha's pill habit a full six months before he thought it necessary to call her attention to it. And he knew about Olivia Abernathy and Dean Van de Sant. He had considered telling the police about their affair in case it could help their investigation, but thought he might need to pull favor with the dean at some point so he changed his mind.

That was part of the game, knowing when to use information. It was like playing the stock market. Sell too soon and you lose. Sell too late and you lose. The best investments are monitored carefully for optimum profit. He had something on Lily Mars too. She'd had an embarrassing issue and made the mistake of taking a call about it in the restroom. He had no idea when he would need to curry a favor from her, but he was sure he would at some point.

He continued fast-forwarding through what amounted to hours of footage. Jared was somewhat heartened by how little dirt he actually did gather on people. Sure, he had his share of nose pickers and cheerleaders passing gas, but he had a standard and would only use evidence of people doing things he thought were actually wrong. Not just human.

William Abernathy appeared on the screen. Jared let the recording slow to real time. Abernathy wasn't alone. And when Jared saw who he was with, everything that had happened in the previous night made total sense to him.

Jared not only understood why Mason killed William Abernathy. He approved.

21. MURDER WEAPON

Van de Sant walked down the hallway near his office, talking to the detectives. He was very pleased with himself.

"I was making my usual rounds this afternoon when I noticed something was askew. Something had not been cleaned properly. Ordinarily, I'd consider this a reason to have a little chat with our cleaning staff. But in this case, I believe their shoddy work can benefit your investigation."

They passed numerous trophy cases jammed with the spoils of a century of the school's successful athletic teams. Gold cups, ribbons, and bronze statues of athletes filled the shelves. Photos dating back to the days when the football team wore what looked like pillows to protect themselves hung on every open surface.

"Danbury has always been one of the better preparatory schools for athletics," Van de Sant explained. "We believe firmly in nurturing our students' minds and bodies equally."

He smiled at the detectives. It was the same spiel he gave to all new families on prospective student tours, though most would apply no matter what he said. Danbury was prestigious and they all wanted prestige. If their athletic program was made up of just synchronized swimming and square dancing, they'd still apply.

The dean and the detectives reached the destination. Another trophy case, but this one was filled with more contemporary awards. Van de Sant pointed out a conspicuously empty section. The shelf was dusty, save for one perfectly clean square spot. Someone had removed a trophy since the last time the cleaning crew had dusted.

"I don't know how long it's been missing."

The detectives seemed unimpressed until Van de Sant threw down his trump card.

"I wouldn't have said anything if it hadn't been his. William's. It seems significant. It was the award William won earlier this year. He wanted to share it with the Danbury community so he asked it be kept here."

He wanted to show it off, Van de Sant thought. The insecure prick wanted everybody to see he'd been honored. He probably was worried Olivia would throw it away if he left it at home. She had impeccable taste, and it was a particularly garish trophy—a crystal column with William Abernathy's name etched in it. FOR EXCELLENCE IN THE COMMUNITY.

"How long ago did he get it?" the younger detective asked, peering at the case.

"About two months, maybe. I can have my assistant get the specific date for you if you'd like. The ceremony was here at Danbury."

"Was it open to the public or by invitation only?"

"We don't ever open anything to the general public." The dean tried to smile kindly at the clueless detective. "This was no exception. It was attended by the usual representatives of the Danbury community. Olivia and both their daughters were there, of course." Van de Sant thought back to the ceremony and party. Alcohol flowed, but only those with addiction issues overindulged. The speeches were witty and warm. Abernathy was surprised, delighted, and humbled, blah, blah, blah. The man had annoyingly straight, white teeth. He must have spent a fortune on dental treatments.

"So William Abernathy was well liked?"

"Mr. Abernathy was very respected in the community," Van de Sant told the detectives. He hoped they were buying his sincerity. "His presence will be sorely missed."

He didn't mention Abernathy and his wife left the event separately. People had no idea what he was capable of. If they knew the truth, he would have been run out of town. The award was ironic at best. Abernathy was anything but a good man. Van de Sant knew it. He bore his own guilt where the man was concerned.

22. WHERE ALL BODIES ARE BURIED

A faint rumbling sound echoed through the empty hallway, bouncing off the plaster walls and polished terrazzo floors. Then, a squeal of delight. Mason ran full throttle, pushing a library cart with Kaylee sitting on top. She was laughing and holding on for deal life as he zigzagged along. "Stop!" she yelled. But she didn't want him to. He pointed the cart toward a water fountain and headed straight for it. Kaylee closed her eyes. "I know you won't hit it. I know you won't!"

She was right. He switched direction at the last minute and then hopped on the back, standing on the bottom shelf. But his weight made it wobble and he had to get off, holding on until the cart slowed to a stop. Kaylee grabbed him and hugged him. "You could've gotten me killed. Or injured, or something. How would I have explained to my parents that I had an accident with a water fountain?"

"You'd just blame me and they'd believe you."

"Good point."

They kissed and Mason lifted her from the cart to standing.

"I love being in the school when it's empty like this." Kaylee walked down the hall, gazing at the glass cases filled with photos, trophies, and plaques from years gone by. There were at least twenty black-and-white pictures of men in baggy knee-length golf pants with huge caps on their heads, standing arm and arm and grinning like idiots. Other pictures showed football players in what passed for padding back in the 1920s. "It makes you realize how old everything is. How much history there is."

"You should see the attic."

"I want to see the attic. I want to see all the secret stuff."

"You should talk to my dad. He knows where all the bodies are buried."

"Really? Like what?"

"I don't know. Just the normal stuff."

"You can't tease me with that and then not give me details."

"Okay. Let me think. Like, you know the French teacher Ms. Melkanoff? She keeps a bottle of schnapps in her desk."

"I thought schnapps was German."

"You're missing the point."

"What else? I need more."

"Mr. Simmons, the Algebra teacher, was having an affair with Miss Campbell. He would leave her love letters in her desk."

"Eeeew. He's like, a gorilla."

"I believe the word is *hirsute.*"

"I thought the word was gross." She leaned over and pushed Mason against the trophy case. "I like that we have the whole place to ourselves. We could do anything, anywhere." They kissed. When she opened her eyes, she focused on something behind him. "Weird."

He turned and followed her gaze. "What?"

"We're making out in front of my dad's award." She pointed to a crystal spike etched with her father's name.

"How was he excellent in the community?" Mason asked as he read the inscription.

"Something to do with brokering a deal to bring a factory to town. And then the school somehow decided since he was a grad here and on the board, they should make a fuss over it."

"That's odd."

"That's my dad."

"Yeah. He's not my favorite person."

"Me neither."

"He fools people, doesn't he? Everybody thinks he's some saint."

"He did help bring the factory to town."

"I wonder how many people he paid off to do it."

"Probably lots."

Mason considered her. "You're pretty great for somebody with such a nutso father."

"Is that right?"

"That is totally right." He took his time kissing her. "You know what I'm going to do?"

Kaylee shook her head.

"I'm going to go get the keys to the attic and show you where the skeletons are hidden." He started to walk away but then turned back. "Real skeletons. I'm not kidding. There's one up there from like, 1943. Wait here."

Kaylee smiled and nodded. When Mason was gone, she turned her attention back to her father's award. She opened the case and took it out, feeling the weight in her hands. After a brief look around, she slipped it into her bag. She had just shut the door to the case as Mason returned.

"You ready to meet Chubby?"

"Chubby?"

"The skeleton."

23. DADDY'S LITTLE GIRL

"So you think someone stole the award and killed William with it?" Olivia sat with Anne. She shook her head. "Can you tell if he defended himself? Did he fight back?"

"We don't know anything yet." The female detective said gently.

"Was it one quick blow or was he beaten?"

"Mom, please." Anne clearly did not like the images that were flashing in her head. "Do we really need to know that?"

"Wouldn't you feel better if you knew it was quick?"

Anne stared at her mother a moment, a response on the tip of her tongue. But she decided to hold back. She turned to the detectives and changed the subject to something less emotionally charged. "If someone used the award to kill my father, that would be significant, right? Like someone was trying to make a point?" Anne asked. Olivia rolled her eyes and interjected, "I'm no expert, but in general, when someone kills someone else, they're making a point."

The two detectives shared a look. People never ceased to surprise them in how they reacted after a tragedy. That was assuming, of course, this woman thought her husband's death was a tragedy.

"The choice of the murder weapon may be significant," the female detective explained, focusing her words toward Anne. "However, we don't have a cause of death yet. Until we have that, we won't have any idea what the murder weapon might have been. If it's determined he was bludgeoned to death, we will absolutely look into who had access to the award. And if it was the award, we will certainly look into why that particular weapon was chosen. It could have been used for convenience. . . ."

"But someone stole it from the case. That's not convenient . . . ," Anne pointed out.

". . . Or it could have been used because someone else wanted the award."

That idea disturbed Olivia on a different level. It was pathetic, really, to think that someone might have been so desperate to win a meaningless award that they took revenge on the winner. If the award was the murder weapon, this was a planned attack, not something someone did in the heat of the moment. Passionate anger seemed less threatening than cold-blooded premeditation. "None of this makes any sense," she told the detectives. "William was well respected and well liked. I don't know of any enemies he had." She didn't say what she was thinking, that she knew of numerous enemies, but none whose identity she was willing to share with the police. He had made many in the business world, but exposing them would mean exposing the family to financial scrutiny, and Olivia did not want that.

"What was Kaylee's relationship like with her father?" the female detective asked.

"Kaylee loved him." Anne piped up. "She would never do this to him."

They had a special relationship, Olivia agreed. "She was Daddy's little girl."

The woman detective shot a glance to see if Anne was hurt by a comment that showed such obvious favoritism. Olivia saw the woman's reaction. "Please don't misunderstand. He loved both his daughters equally. Both were Daddy's little girl. It's just that Kaylee enjoyed the attention more than Anne."

Anne nodded. "It's okay. Kaylee was his favorite. I know that. He was still a good father to me."

"We've heard that your father didn't approve of the relationship with Mason. Do you think it's possible they did this to him?"

Both Olivia and Anne shook their heads.

"Kaylee would never do this," Anne said. "And Mason would do what Kaylee said."

"Mason is not her puppy. He has a mind of his own," Olivia insisted. "I know you think he's devoted to your sister, and I don't doubt he is to some degree, but you can't ignore the fact that he has a temper. And he's smart. Smart enough to get that statue and hold on to it until the time was right."

Anne shook her head. She couldn't believe her mother was trying to pin this on Mason when she knew of a much more obvious choice. Olivia was feigning ignorance. Who could be more obvious than Mason? She stared at her daughter blankly, but Anne knew her mind was racing. She was willing her to keep silent. Anne had to hand it to her, her mother was brilliant at maintaining a facade. The thing was, she was tired of the facade.

"My mother hated my father," Anne told the police. "She was cheating on him."

24. HER FACE SCREAMED GUILT!

Glinda was a bit disappointed her big revelation didn't get more of a reaction from the detectives. Her info was *primo fantastico* considering who the dead guy was, but these two took it in stride.

"How did you know Mrs. Abernathy was having an affair?" The younger detective smiled in encouragement. He seemed to like Glinda more than the old dude. It didn't surprise her. Old dudes generally didn't approve of her hair. Or her nails. Or her shoes. Or her personality.

"I was cutting class a few months back. When I do that I usually just wander around the school. My mom would say I was looking for trouble, but really I was looking for entertainment. Anything out of the ordinary, you know? When I cut, it's usually to get out of English Lit. My teacher, Miss White, so appropriately named, by the way, does not have a creative bone in her brittle little body. The woman wears the same outfit every single day of the year, in different colors: tweed jacket, blouse, skirt, and sensible low-heeled shoes. She's a crime against vision. Anyway. She wants us to write essays the same way she dresses, boring, with the exact same structure every time."

"About the affair?"

"Right. On that particular day, I'd excused myself to use the restroom, and then decided to take a walk. I was on the administrative area of the school, right outside where we are now. It was during class, so the hall was empty. The door to Dean Van de Sant's office opened and out walked Kaylee's mom."

"Why was that surprising?"

"In itself, it's no big deal to see a parent coming out of the dean's office, her in particular. She's one of those ladies who lunch, you know? She's on every board and committee. She might have loads of reasons to meet with the dean. But I could tell this wasn't about some committee."

"How so?"

"When she saw me, the look that flashed on her face screamed *Guilt!* And she was smoothing her hair. It had been mussed. You know? Not messy. Mussed." Glinda said the last word with a salacious tone.

"Did you say anything to her?"

"What was I going to say? 'Was it good for you?' I didn't say anything to her and she didn't say anything to me. She just got her game face back on and walked by me. I turned to watch her leave. She had a serious strut going, like the hallway was a runway and her dress was part of the new spring collection. Which it wasn't."

The younger detective gave a little cough to get Glinda back on track.

"Right. So I'm watching her, and then, behind me, the dean opened the door. He was tucking in his shirt." Glinda demonstrated what she meant. "He may as well have been zipping his fly." She laughed at the memory. "He was a little out of breath and looked positively perturbed when he saw me. 'Shouldn't you be in class, young lady, getting an education?' He asked, all uptight." Glinda did a fair job of mimicking Van de Sant's formal cadence.

"What did you tell him?" the younger detective asked.

"I told him I was getting an education at that very moment. I knew way more than I had a few minutes before."

The dean's eye twitched a little when she'd said that. Ever since then, she'd made sure to give him a wink every time she saw him.

"Yes. I was having an affair with the dead man's wife," Van de Sant said with resignation, maintaining his best poker face. He vowed to expel that little monstrosity Glinda the first chance he got. If she so much as littered, he'd boot her. "I realize the implication."

What an implication it was. Of all the people to get murdered, it had to be his mistress's husband. Van de Sant knew it looked bad, but he told the detectives the truth. "I did not kill William Abernathy. While Olivia and I are involved, you must understand there is no ill will among the parties. *Was* no ill will. Bill Abernathy was an agreeable cuckold, one might say. Cuckold in that he was being cheated on."

"Is that what cuckold means? Gee. I didn't know." The older detective's voice dripped sarcasm.

"He knew his wife had outside relationships. Bill and Olivia had what some might call an open marriage. Please, ask Olivia about the specifics of their agreement. I personally preferred not to hear the details. Olivia and I have been discreet, certainly, but not because of fear of discovery by spouses. We were much more concerned with keeping up appearances in the community."

"Of course."

The detective was being adversarial and Van de Sant bristled, but he had to make his case. "Why would I provide you with details about what might be the murder weapon if I were the guilty party? Surely you realize how illogical that would be."

"Where were you last night?" the younger detective asked.

Van de Sant nodded. Finally, a relevant question. "I was with Olivia. At the EconoLodge off I-Ninety-Five." The older detective's face was still, but Van de Sant knew he was judging the choice of accommodations. "Olivia likes it there. We, of course, could go to my home, but a hotel provides a certain anonymity that can be freeing." Olivia liked a lot of things he didn't feel the need to share. When he told them about the affair, he thought the detectives might have been a bit impressed. Olivia was a fine specimen of womanhood. Just thinking about her taut body sent a pleasing current through him.

He was at her mercy really. The affair had already put him in a compromising position and made him shirk professional responsibility, but he couldn't bring himself to break it off. Mason Henry should be grateful to Olivia. She's the only reason he was still a student on campus and not some gangster's punching bag in a public school. When Mason attacked Jared Slater, Van de Sant was ready to punish him. It would've been standard. But Mason's father had come to him and told him if he kicked Mason out, he would leak the affair between him and Olivia. It was blackmail, pure and simple. Olivia would have been embarrassed by the disclosure, but Van de Sant would have been ruined. The Danbury board of trustees would have fired him. He was good at his job and they respected that, but he was not one of them. Sleeping with someone in their social strata would not be tolerated.

"Why are you even bothering to dredge up this nonsense?" Van de Sant looked at the detectives. "Isn't it obvious who killed Bill? Surely you don't think it's a coincidence that Mason and Kaylee ran away the same night her father was murdered?"

25. WE WEREN'T SCHOOLGIRLS

Olivia watched Anne leave the room after her great declaration about Olivia having an affair. What a little bitch. Olivia knew she wasn't particularly close with her daughters, but that revelation was really uncalled for.

She turned back to the detectives. "My husband and I have an arrangement. We are, were, good friends who no longer felt the passion of a new relationship, but we didn't want to divorce and break up our family."

"So you had affairs?" The older detective seemed completely nonplussed.

"Basically, yes."

"So your husband, he was having affairs too?"

"I'm sure he wasn't celibate."

"Who was he sleeping with?"

"I have no idea," Olivia replied with scorn. "We had an agreement. We weren't schoolgirls sharing details about our latest crushes."

"Did he know about your relationship with Jeremy Van de Sant?"

"Maybe, but I don't think so. We've been discreet." Olivia thought briefly of that odd student, Glinda, who saw her coming out of Jeremy's office. She surely suspected something, but she wouldn't have told William. "Detectives, I don't want to tell you how to do your job, but you should be focusing on finding Mason and Kaylee. I want my daughter home safely."

"We're doing everything we can, ma'am," the older detective assured her.

"What does that mean? Do you have any leads? Any suspects?"

The detectives let the last question hang in the air. Olivia immediately knew what they were thinking.

"Any real suspects?" she clarified. "Other than Mason and Kaylee?"

"We're considering all evidence."

"Do you have fingerprints? Have you checked the car?"

"The car was wiped clean."

"That's unfortunate." Olivia's voice dripped sincerity. No fingerprints on the car—that certainly made the case more difficult for them to solve.

Anne smiled, thinking about the look on her mother's face when Anne told the police about her affair. She was shocked and offended. Anne didn't know if her mother didn't realize her daughter knew, or if she thought she'd keep it a secret. Secrets were so important in their family. Her mother probably took it for granted that Anne wouldn't talk. She never thought she'd say or do anything controversial. What was she always calling her? Oatmeal? "So bland it's practically inedible." Kaylee had snapped at Olivia the last time she insulted Anne like that. She'd be so pleased that Anne outed their mother to the cops. She was always telling Anne to fight back.

Olivia had insisted to the police she couldn't answer any questions about her relationship with Jeremy Van de Sant in front of Anne. She was just a child, after all. "She's had enough to deal with for one day."

Anne was excused from the questioning. She quietly snuck into Kaylee's bedroom. A giant Navajo-print *K* hung over the bed. The rest of the room was not much different from Anne's. Olivia had hired a designer a few years ago to redo the house and had insisted the two bedrooms have a unified look. Kaylee and Anne were annoyed, but in the end, they had similar tastes so it wasn't that big of a deal. They did insist on personalizing them despite Olivia's protests. She wanted something magazine-spread ready. The rooms were at first, until Kaylee added some of her favorite photos in little frames on the wall and scattered colorful pillows about. Anne took down some of the art the designer had chosen in her room. The woman had gone for a French theme and had framed photographs of Parisian landmarks hung in perfect symmetry on the walls. It felt kind of, well, oatmealy. Kaylee would laugh at that.

Anne knew her sister wouldn't leave without saying goodbye. It just wasn't like her. She checked under Kaylee's bed. She had a box where she kept her favorite mementos. Anne smiled as she sorted through them—ticket stubs from a boy-band concert they'd gone to years ago, a dog-eared copy of *To Kill a Mockingbird*, several spent glow sticks. Kaylee went through a glowstick phase a while back, largely for Anne's entertainment. She would make them into various shapes like some people make balloon animals.

But no note. No message. *Think*, she told herself. If Kaylee were going to leave something for you, where would she leave it?

The answer hit her. She got up and went to Kaylee's bathroom and opened one of the drawers and pulled out a box of tampons. When she and Kaylee wanted to keep things from their dad, they'd always put them inside. It was the one place he would never look.

She took the box and dumped it on the bed. Sticking out of the pile of tampons was a note. Score!

ANNA BANANA.

IF YOU'RE READING THIS, IT
MEANS I'M GONE. I'M SURE YOU
KNOW WHY I HAD TO LEAVE. I'M
SORRY. I'LL BE BACK FOR YOU.
BE READY.

LOVE, K.

26. BALLS LIKE AN ELEPHANT

Mason waited as William Abernathy got the extra money from the safe. He heard his own heart pumping in his ears. He was furious that the prick was trying to break up him and Kaylee, but pleased at how he'd managed to turn the situation to his own advantage. He thought back to the night he found out Kaylee's father was cheating on his wife. It was after he won the community award. The crowd had cleared and Mason was loading folding chairs into a truck out back. He heard something get knocked over and noticed a couple practically humping each other behind the building. That in itself wasn't anything noteworthy, but then he saw the statue on the ground. A crystal spiky thing. He couldn't see the man's face, but he knew the award belonged to Kaylee's father.

Mason moved closer. Kaylee had gone home with her mother, so whoever the respected Danbury citizen was urgently grinding into wasn't his wife. Of course Mason wanted to see who it was. He assumed it would be one of the area's huge pool of bored wives and mothers, affluent women who needed to create drama to escape the hollow repetitiveness of days spent shopping and lunching. Mason hoped it was Jared Slater's mom. That would upend that asshat's world.

It felt almost wrong to watch two people going at it so passionately, but it was worth the wait. When Abernathy came up for air, Mason immediately recognized her. She was definitely someone known to the Danbury community, but she was not an aging socialite. Kaylee's dad was screwing around with a student at Danbury. Mason thought about Kaylee and how she would react if she knew and immediately decided not to tell her.

Mason looked up as Abernathy returned to the living room with a bigger pile of money. He slid it across the table at Mason. The man was so cocky. He viewed people like objects he could buy and sell. He didn't follow rules himself, but he expected others to obey the ones he set.

"I expect you'll break up with her tonight. Tomorrow at the latest."

Mason shook his head as he took the money and fanned it. He'd never seen that much cash. "Here's the thing. I'm not breaking up with Kaylee."

"If you don't break up with Kaylee, I will report that you stole that money. I didn't have to offer you anything."

"Add *generous* to all those great things people think about you."

"You don't seem to understand the power I have in this town." Abernathy was fighting to maintain his composure.

"You have balls like an elephant, I'll give you that," Mason told him. "To lecture me about how I'm not good enough for your little girl when you're fucking one of her friends. Her underage friend."

Abernathy stayed perfectly still as Mason continued. "I know about you and Lily." He thought back to the night of the award. When Abernathy and his macking partner came up for air, Mason could see he'd had Lily Mars pinned against the wall. Lily had pulled him back to her, wanting more.

Mason grinned across the table at Abernathy. He enjoyed seeing this snob try to figure out how to regain the upper hand knowing full well that he couldn't. It wasn't often Mason could use his words and still feel like he was winning a fight. "I don't know much about the law, but I'm guessing it's one of those crimes you go to jail for. You think you'd like jail? You think your connections would help you inside? Maybe get you cigarettes or some extra time in the yard?"

"You have no proof of anything."

"Maybe. Maybe not. But I'm betting proof exists somewhere. Phone records. Text messages. Love notes." Abernathy paled. He'd covered his tracks, but apparently not that well. How did this little shit know? He wondered if Lily had bragged to someone.

Mason didn't stop. "Just the accusation would do serious damage. What would your wife do? Your kids? You think people want to do business with an accused pedophile?"

"She's not a child."

"So you're admitting it."

Abernathy couldn't believe how badly things had turned. He thought he was buying off a problem, and here he was getting extorted. "What do you want?"

Mason rose and pocketed the pile of cash. His wish was very simple.

"I love your daughter. I'm going to be with her. Don't try and stop me again."

<center>~~~</center>

Jared thought of the image he saw on his laptop, of Lily Mars and his mentor, William Abernathy, going at it in the bathroom. He felt sick to his stomach, not only because the man had shown himself to be so immoral, but because Jared realized there was a much greater implication, one that could provide an entirely new light on the murder.

But first he told the detectives about Lily.

"I believe Mr. Abernathy was involved with one of the students here. Lily Mars."

It was the first time the detectives visibly reacted to anything he'd said.

"You have proof?"

"No, but I know I'm right." Of course he couldn't tell them he was secretly recording people throughout the school. He thought it might be illegal, and at the very least, he worried about jeopardizing the elaborate system he had in place. The detectives prodded him, trying to get him to reveal his source. But Jared held fast. He needed to explain to them that Mr. Abernathy sleeping with Lily wasn't even the biggest shock.

Lily stared at the detectives, unflinching and unapologetic.

"He loved me."

Lily was grieving. She had something special with Will. They both knew people wouldn't understand. They would frown on the age difference. Ordinary people couldn't see what Will did, that Lily was unusually mature for her age. She was an old soul in a young body. They could talk for hours about everything. When she was with him, Lily felt unbelievably light.

She fought back tears as she thought of when they first discovered their feelings for each other. It was over a year ago. Lily was stretched out by the Abernathy pool one day after school. She soaking up the sun in a retro, '70s-style bikini with a giant O ring at the cleavage. Kaylee had gone inside to use the bathroom or who knows what. William Abernathy came outside from his bedroom. The house was U-shaped and several rooms opened out onto the pool. He nodded hello at Lily and continued past her to the kitchen. When he came back, he was holding some sort of green juice. Again, he walked by her, but something made him stop. "I don't want to be rude, but do I know you?" Lily smiled.

"I've only been here like a million times." He still looked perplexed. Lily took off her sunglasses. "It's Lily. Lily Mars."

"Lily Mars is a little girl who wants to be a princess when she grows up."

"I can't believe you remembered that. That was like, ten years ago."

"You don't want to be a princess anymore?"

"Maybe I already am a princess."

"Don't sell yourself short. You clearly have way too many smarts to settle for that."

"So what will I be then?"

"I have a pretty strong feeling you can be whatever you want."

He'd continued to his room then. Lily watched him go, a bit surprised. Boys of any age rarely would leave her alone, particularly when she was in a bikini. But he seemed unimpressed by her body.

At least at first. That afternoon was the start of something. Lily made it a point to hang out with Kaylee more often so she could "accidentally" bump into her father. It didn't take long for her to "accidentally" show up at the house when Kaylee wasn't there.

She knew the detectives were judging him harshly because of their relationship. People would. It was why they were waiting until Lily turned eighteen to go public. At that point, Will would leave Olivia and marry her. Kaylee and Anne would have a hard time accepting it, but they didn't care. Love knew no bounds.

And now he was dead. She had no future and never felt so alone in her life.

"Where were you last night between nine and midnight?" The older detective didn't care about her pain.

"I was at the party at Keesha's house. Everybody saw me."

27.THE PARTY

Every window in Keesha Washington's modern house glowed brightly as the party gained momentum. People spilled from room to room. The wide second-floor balcony was filled with Danbury students sipping from red cups. Keesha had decided to go old school for the evening and was pushing gin and tonics with a twist of lime. Her favorite band, Trick Knee, was playing over the home's audio system. It was loud enough to hear, but not so loud that it was impossible to have a conversation. Keesha was very aware it was her duty as hostess to make sure all guests were having a good time, and all the guests were being respectful of her home.

Her parents were in Turks and Caicos celebrating their twentieth wedding anniversary. They'd trusted Keesha to stay by herself and even told her she could have a get-together if she wanted. They knew they could trust their daughter. What they didn't realize was that their daughter was, at that moment, standing outside near the curb of the house waiting for her dealer to show up. Still, pills or not, she would make sure no one damaged anything during the party.

Keesha was standing there when Kaylee arrived. "Have you seen Mason?" No "Hello" or anything resembling a friendly greeting.

Keesha tried not to be hurt. "Didn't he bring you?" Mason always brought Kaylee. They were inseparable.

"He was supposed to, but he never showed. I don't know what's going on. I'm worried about him."

Keesha nodded sympathetically. "Why don't you go look inside?"

Kaylee nodded and left without another word. *Nice*, Keesha thought. But honestly, she wanted her gone. She needed to be alone.

Kaylee headed through the throngs of people, scanning the crowd. People were dancing, groping, and generally having a good time. She felt so apart from it all. She spotted Trevor hitting on an older guy, probably a college kid. When she approached, he hugged her hello. "Have you seen Lily? She's already half past gone." Trevor gestured to the dance floor, where Lily was working her best moves but looking like an awkward marionette. "Some people get drunk and make unfortunate moves on other people. Lily gets drunk and makes unfortunate moves on the dance floor." Trevor waited for Kaylee to laugh, but she wasn't even listening.

"Have you seen Mason?" Trevor shook his head. "Didn't you come with him?"

But she left without answering. Trevor turned his attention back to the delicious-looking frat boy he'd been hitting on, but he was gone now too. Just his luck.

Kaylee made her way through the throngs. She nearly ran straight into Jared. He smiled warmly when he saw her. "Kaylee. I was hoping to see you here." He took a step forward, but she held up a hand to keep him at bay. "I'm sorry, Jared, but not now."

She spotted Mason across the room, around the Ping-Pong table doing shots with a few other people. He looked right at her but didn't smile or acknowledge her in any way. She turned and headed outside, not sure what to do next. She couldn't stay here with him ignoring her. She headed down the back way toward the street when Mason grabbed her arm. She smiled at him instinctively, but the angry look in his eyes made her pull back. "Where were you? Why didn't you pick me up?"

Mason seemed almost too angry to speak. He took her by the arm and guided her away from the partiers. He somehow managed to make a whisper sound menacing. "I know you cheated on me."

"What? That's crazy."

"Don't lie to me."

"I'm not lying."

"Who was it?"

"I didn't cheat with anybody."

"Just tell me, okay? Tell me who it was. Was it that prick Jared?"

"No! Of course not. What is this about? I never cheated on you."

"My dick says otherwise."

Kaylee paused for the slightest second, but Mason saw. "I knew it," he said.

"No. Stop. It's not what you think." Kaylee was getting louder and louder, unable to keep her emotions in check. "I did not cheat on you."

"You had to. I've never cheated on you. Not once. I don't even look at anybody else. What's that phrase? I only had eyes for you. And look what it got me."

"You don't understand what's been happening."

"I know exactly what's been happening, and what's going to happen. We're through."

"No! You have to believe me."

"I'll believe you when you tell me who you slept with."

"I didn't."

"I don't ever want to see you again."

Mason started walking back toward the house. Kaylee followed. She caught him by the arm, and he shook her off so roughly she flinched.

"We're done here. Do not follow me." He kept walking and Kaylee took another step toward him as he turned. "If you follow me, I swear to God I'll kill you." With that, Mason headed inside. As he was walking, he almost ran into Glinda.

Once again Kaylee started to go after him, but Trevor had been watching and stepped in to block her. "No, sweetie. It's not a good idea."

"I can't believe this is happening." Kaylee was sobbing. "What am I going to do?"

"Wait. He'll calm down."

"And then what? Tell him the truth? What will happen then?"

"What exactly is the truth?"

"You know."

"I think. But I don't know. If I knew I'd have to do something about it."

"You can't."

"I want to help you."

"Nobody can help me. Nobody would believe me."

"That's not true."

"It would follow me forever. I'd be that girl. You know, 'the one who.'" Kaylee was worried that she would get a reputation if people knew where she really got it. It wasn't her fault, but that didn't matter. She didn't want any story about her sex life following her.

"Come with me. We can figure something out." He led her toward the street.

"I know what I want to do."

"I know what I want to do too."

28. I'M THE COWARD?

Mason went inside the house and grabbed another shot of vodka. He downed it without even feeling the sting in his throat. He looked at all the faces around him. Some were staring and others were pretending not to look. Screw them. He felt his neck get hot as he thought about what just happened. He couldn't believe it. He loved Kaylee and she cheated on him.

He hit the head. As he was standing there, Lily walked in. Stumbled, really. She didn't seem embarrassed he had his dick in his hands, positioned over the toilet. She walked toward him and reached for it. Mason blocked her, the crazy bitch.

"What do you think you're doing?"

"I'm just saying hello," Lily slurred her words. "I saw you fight with Kaylee. So now you're free, right?"

"Right."

"So? What are we waiting for?"

"Lily. You're drunk."

"Absolutely."

"I thought you had a boyfriend."

"Do you see a boyfriend anywhere?"

"I know who your boyfriend is."

Lily froze. "What do you mean?"

"You know what I mean. I know who your boyfriend is. The 'mature' guy. Otherwise known as the creep who could go to jail for diddling his daughter's friend."

"He's not diddling me."

Mason zipped up his pants. "You realize he's using you, right?"

"Of course you'd think that."

"Jesus, Lily. Do you hear yourself?"

"Did you tell anyone? Any adults?"

"Adults besides your boyfriend? No. But I will if you don't turn around and leave me in peace."

"You little roach."

"Leave me in peace. You don't want to do this."

Mason took his time washing his hands, making it a point to ignore Lily. He walked past her and out the door. Lily fumed. She couldn't believe she'd offered herself to him. She wasn't even sure why she did. Something about Kaylee having the attention of Mason and her own boyfriend really bugged her.

Mason was so angry and upset about Kaylee that he barely registered what had just happened in the bathroom. If he'd thought about it, he'd have known Lily wouldn't handle rejection all that well. But he didn't think. He wanted to get the hell away from this party so he pushed his way through the crowd and to the door.

He was already in his car, about to pull the door shut, when *BAM!* Jared yanked the door open.

"What the hell?"

"You crossed the line this time." Jared pulled Mason out of the car and tossed him to the street. Mason scrambled to his feet as Jared kept at him. "You're messing with her. You coward."

"Coward?" Mason faked a lunge toward Jared. He flinched. "Got it. I'm the coward."

Sarcasm dripped from Mason's voice.

"We both know what's going on with you and Kaylee."

"Oh, yeah? You know? You gangly prick. You don't know anything."

"I know you've been cheating on her."

Mason lunged for real this time. He pinned Jared against the Mustang. "I'm sick of you and this shit about me and Kaylee. You think she's so fantastic? Take a shot at her."

"You're an asshole."

"She's free. Unattached. On the market."

Jared pushed back. He used his height to tower over Mason, trying to intimidate him. "You dumped her? It figures. You ruin her, and then you throw her away. You're not even man enough to own it."

"I'm trying really hard here not to grind that pretty face of yours into the ground." Mason tried to walk around Jared to get into his car, but Jared wasn't about to let him go.

"You're not getting away with it. "

"Get out of my way."

"You're not going to claim she cheated on you when you were the one who cheated."

"I never cheated on Kaylee. Not once."

"We both know where you got it."

"Good. I'm glad we both know! Ask me again if I care about whatever fiction you've created about my life!"

"You screwed around with Lily, and you're trying to blame Kaylee for what you caught."

Mason stopped. Something was connecting in his head. "Lily? What are you talking about?"

"You screwed around with Lily. You caught it from her and you gave it to Kaylee."

"Lily has it?"

"Play dumb. It's not too far from the truth. If you were faithful, how would Kaylee have caught something? You think she's screwing around with somebody else? We both know she's not like that. Her only flaw is that she was foolish enough to trust you and be faithful to you."

Mason thought back to the night Kaylee's father won the community award, when he saw him going at it with Lily. Lily caught something. Kaylee caught the same thing, then gave it to Mason. Only one person was the link between them.

Mason pushed past Jared and got into his car. He put it in gear and peeled out, nearly running over a girl leaving the party. He drove without thought at first, not sure where he should go. Everything that had happened in the previous months suddenly made more sense, like he was seeing his past through new glasses— Kaylee worrying about what secret he had on her father. Her being freaked out the first time they had sex. The bruises on her arm that didn't make sense. It was right in front of him. Kaylee was suffering and he didn't see it.

He swerved to the side of the road and threw open the car door with barely enough time to stick his head out and retch. He heaved with such force it felt like his intestines were going to come out with the rest of his stomach contents. He threw up guilt and agony for what Kaylee had been going through until nothing came up anymore. He felt shaky as he forced himself to think. Obviously, he had to get to her. He had to make sure she was safe. He couldn't believe he'd broken up with Kaylee over this. What she must be going through. What she'd been through. It made him sick and angry.

Then, a different thought started to form. He had to get to her father. To make sure he never hurt her again. It was the only obvious thing to do.

He was running on pure rage by the time he got to Kaylee's house. He was going to find her father and make him suffer for what he'd done. Mason parked and made his way to the garage. He used his pocket knife to swiftly disable the flimsy lock.

He pulled open the door, planning to sneak into the house and surprise the man.

But when he opened it, he found William Abernathy in the garage. Dead, on the ground, in a puddle of his own blood. His face and head were mangled, but there was no denying who he was. Kaylee had beaten him to it. Mason wasn't sure whose fault it was. Her father's certainly, but Mason felt responsible. He had broken up with her over something that was clearly a result of her being victimized. He pushed her to the edge. Mason had not thought her capable of such a thing. He would've sworn otherwise. But maybe that was what attracted her to him, he realized. Maybe she had a deep, hidden anger and was drawn to him because his anger was right there, on the surface, waiting to come up. Or maybe she wanted somebody who could protect her. He wished he had.

A car drove by outside, startling Mason. He quickly got inside the garage and shut the door. He stared at the body, thinking.

He had to help her somehow. This was a mess. Hiding the body at least would buy them some time. Mason pulled his jacket off and looked around for some tarps, or blankets, or anything he could use to wrap it.

It was tough work, but adrenaline fueled him. He laid the blanket down and then managed to lift the body onto it, rolling it like a human burrito. Mason didn't have room in his own trunk to transport it. He could hardly leave the contents of his car trunk here and take the body. He considered his options, then went over and opened the trunk of William Abernathy's white Mercedes.

29.WE NEED TO GO

He was tucking a clean blanket over the body when he got a text from Kaylee: **Goodbye, Mason. I really did love you.**

Holy shit. He slammed the trunk shut. What was Kaylee doing? What an idiot he'd been. He focused on the body when he should have been focused on her.

He grabbed his jacket and headed up the stairs from the garage into the house.

He moved quietly, not sure who else was home. He didn't want to run into Kaylee's mother or Anne and have to explain what he was doing there.

He moved past the kitchen and saw Kaylee out by the pool. She was sitting at the water's edge, holding a knife to her wrist. Jesus. No! He rushed out to her, startling her as he yanked the knife away.

"What are you doing?"

"Nothing. I was just thinking." She was dazed and had a faraway air about her.

"Don't ever think that," he said. "Nothing is so bad as that."

"Things are a mess, Mason."

Mason took her hands in his. "Promise me you will never hurt yourself."

Kaylee shook her head. "I don't think I can."

"Promise me."

Kaylee whispered it. "I won't hurt myself." Mason knew she was just appeasing him.

"Promise me."

Kaylee stared at him, not giving in. She seemed to remember the events of earlier in the night. His accusations. Their breakup. His threat.

"Why are you here? What else is there to say? You think I cheated. I get it. Don't make it any harder."

Mason wasn't sure how to proceed. She seemed so fragile. He didn't want to make things worse. But he realized he didn't have time to go too slowly.

"I know about your father."

Kaylee's eyes widened. "What about him?"

"Everything."

"That doesn't narrow it down." Kaylee wasn't looking at him.

"I know what he did to you."

Kaylee let this sink in. She was silent. Mason waited. He gingerly touched her shoulder, and his touch seemed to open the dam for her.

"I'm sorry. I'm so sorry." She started to cry.

He wrapped his arms around her. "Stop. Don't say that."

"I didn't cheat on you. I swear."

Mason shook his head. In the middle of all this, she was still worried about hurting him. "I know."

"I would never cheat on you. I couldn't tell you."

Mason pulled her back to look in her eyes. "You can tell me anything. From now on. You tell me anything. We'll figure it out. We'll figure out what to do. You understand that?"

Kaylee pulled in close again. "I didn't know what to do." She looked down at her hand and saw blood from where she'd touched him. "Oh my God. You're hurt."

Mason shook his head. "It's not mine." Kaylee looked confused. "I saw him. In the garage."

"You saw my father?" She was alarmed. Mason nodded.

"I put his body in the trunk of the car."

Kaylee couldn't seem to shake the fog around her. "What do you mean?"

"I mean, I wrapped his body up in some old sheets and blankets, and put it in the trunk of his car."

"His body?"

"His body."

Kaylee slowly processed what he meant. Mason could see the exact moment when she fully understood. "You did that for me?"

"There's nothing I wouldn't do for you. You understand that? Nothing."

"He can't hurt me anymore? It's over?"

Mason knew it was far from over. "We need to go."

"But if he's dead, why?"

"Because he's dead." Mason's voice was urgent. "And they'll want to know who did it."

He realized Kaylee was thinking the abuse was over, so she had no reason to go. She hadn't begun to understand that her actions had changed everything. If she stayed here, the police would come for her. There would be a trial. Everything would come out. People certainly would understand why she killed her father, but that might not get her out of serving time.

Mason pulled her to standing. "We're gonna go pack some of your things."

"I'm scared," she whispered.

"I'm not going to let anybody hurt you. Ever again. I know things seem very bad. But we're not going to think of it that way." Mason wiped the runny mascara from under her eyes. "You're going to remember tonight as the night that you took control of your life. This is not a bad night. This is a good night. He is never going to touch you. . . ."

Kaylee yanked away from him, the fog momentarily lifted.

"Stop. Stop it. I don't want to talk about it. Ever. Don't say it. Don't mention it. I don't want to think about it. Ever."

"You don't have to do anything you don't want ever again," Mason spoke calmly. "We need to go. Now. Let's get your things."

He guided her through the living room, down the hall to her bedroom. He grabbed a black tote bag and dumped some drawers on the bed, randomly grabbing underwear and shirts and stuffing them in the bag. Kaylee disappeared into her bathroom.

"What are you doing?"

"I need to write Anne a note. I don't want to leave her."

"She'll be okay. She's safe. And the less she knows, the better for her."

30. I HAD TO DO IT

Kaylee leaned against the Mustang's window, watching the lights outside flash by. The events of the night, of the weeks and months before, were too much to handle.

"He deserved it. Don't ever think for a minute that he didn't," Mason said as he gripped the steering wheel. She nodded without turning to look at him.

Kaylee had no idea where they were at the moment. Industrial-looking buildings blurred into one another as the Mustang raced along a highway, going fast but not over the speed limit. Mason knew enough not to risk getting caught. He had taken charge and Kaylee willingly followed him. She vaguely remembered packing and leaving her sister a note.

After an hour, when they were far outside the city, Mason exited the interstate and pulled into a gas station. He used cash to tank up, careful to keep his head down in case there were cameras anywhere. Kaylee ventured into the women's restroom. She barely noticed the smell as she leaned on the white porcelain sink and stared in the mirror. She felt odd that the face staring back at her was exactly as it had always been. Somehow, she'd expected it to be different. She felt so different inside.

When she got back in the car, Mason was already waiting. He offered her a granola bar, but she couldn't even think of eating. When they pulled out of the gas station, they drove under the interstate overpass and headed toward the dark hills ahead of them. Streetlights were few and far between, and houses even less so. Deep woods bordered the two-lane road and eventually it seemed like they were far from humanity.

After what seemed like forever, Mason pulled to the side of the road where the forest had cleared.

"We're high up," Kaylee said. The road had been ascending and they now had a view of the valley. Moonlight cast a faint glow over it all. It would have been romantic in any other circumstance.

"Give me your phone." Mason held out his hand. She gave it to him without questioning. He was so sure of himself. It was what had always attracted her to him. He didn't let people take advantage of him. Kaylee needed that in her life.

When he took the phone, he threw it on the ground and stomped it with his boot.

"They could use this to trace us." He took the shattered phone and hurled it into the valley, and then he did the same with his own. "We'll get burner phones later."

"I don't have anybody's numbers memorized. They were all stored."

"We'll figure it out. Don't worry."

"My pictures too."

"I had to do it. You understand that, right?"

She thought he was talking about more than the phone.

"I know."

He climbed back into the car and made a U-turn.

"Are we going back?"

"We're just doubling back a little. I want to throw the cops off our trail."

Kaylee watched him as he drove. He looked tired and wired at the same time. On some level, she thought that everything had been leading to this moment, or these circumstances, for a long time. She remembered the first time they'd talked, outside the dean's office. What Mason didn't realize, what she'd never told him, was that she was attracted to him before that day. She'd seen him on campus, working with his father, arguing in the hallway with other students over something in the news. He stood out. He didn't care what people thought. That was attractive for sure, but not because she wanted to be with someone rebellious. She still had a hard time explaining it, even to herself. She was drawn to him because she hoped, on some level, he was strong enough to handle all there was to know about her. He didn't have years of upper-class social training that told him to keep private matters private, to not complain no matter how bad the situation was. He wasn't raised to find denial soothing.

What she hadn't expected was how sweet he could be when no one was looking. He was so tough, but so gentle with her. She thought of their nightly web chats. He could comfort her and make her laugh at herself at the same time.

Even now, as they drove away from the mess they left in Danbury, she could identify the one thing she felt for the first time in years. Safe.

31. AFTER THE INTERROGATIONS

Trevor, Glinda, and Keesha sat in the hallway outside the dean's office while Jared paced nearby. As far as they knew, the police questioning was done, but no one felt ready to leave. It had been a day of one revelation after the other, each worse than the last.

"It can't be true." Jared shook his head. "They're lying to get us to say more."

Trevor shook his head. "Please, give it a rest. It's true."

"So you knew?" Keesha leaned forward to face him. She couldn't believe what he was saying. Trevor got defensive. "Not exactly."

But he'd said enough. She was disgusted. "And you didn't do anything?"

"I didn't know for sure." Trevor thought back to various conversations he'd had with Kaylee. She never told him anything specific, but he sensed something different about her in recent years. She was darker, more melancholy. It had coincided at least in part with the start of their high school years. He'd thought it might just be the crazy hormones everybody always talked about in Health Ed.

It was only after she'd asked him to check between her legs a few months ago he knew something was seriously wrong. She never once accused Mason of giving it to her. Trevor had wondered who the real culprit was, but she refused to say. He'd assumed she'd been forced to do something she didn't want, but he had no idea by whom.

Jared stopped in front of him, his long frame tense. "But you suspected and you didn't do anything to help her?"

"If I knew, I would have done something."

"You did know," Keesha said it almost to herself.

"Coward!" Jared spat.

"Maybe I was." Trevor vowed to himself that he wouldn't be in the future. If he could help Kaylee somehow, he would. He looked down at the text he'd just received. It was from Anne. **Meet me outside my house.** It might be at least one small way to help redeem himself. He stood and exited down the hall, passing Lily as she came out of the bathroom. She'd been crying. Keesha and Jared looked away, but Glinda stared at her, smirking.

"I'm sorry for your loss."

"Don't judge me, you little toad." Lily seethed.

"Ribbit." Glinda was enjoying Lily's discomfort.

"How can she not judge you?" Jared asked. "Jesus. He's married. And old."

"He did not love his wife."

Keesha snorted. "He loved you?"

"Yes." Lily knew it sounded ridiculous as soon as she said it, but she believed it. She refused to believe everything they'd shared was false.

"You and Kaylee, apparently," Glinda added.

"That is a vicious lie somebody started."

Jared shook his head. "Right."

"I can't believe this is happening." Keesha was feeling nauseated.

"Nothing is happening to you," Lily admonished her.

"Everything is happening to everybody. What is wrong with you?" Keesha moved toward Lily, her hands clenched at her side.

"Oooh. Good girl gets angry!"

Keesha spun toward Glinda. "Shut up, you . . . freak!"

Her classmates froze. No one had ever seen Keesha lose her calm composure, let alone call names. Once she started, she wasn't prepared to stop.

"This isn't funny," she addressed all of them. "There is nothing funny about this. It's sick and tragic and sad and you all are so concerned about yourselves you're not thinking of Kaylee and what all this must have been like for her."

Lily couldn't let that go. "He did not hurt Kaylee."

"Because he was with you?" Jared was incredulous. "That means nothing."

"Because he wouldn't do that."

"Give it a rest, Lily." Keesha fumed. "If he was screwing you he was already crazy. What kind of adult does that with his daughter's friend?"

"One that likes them young." Glinda smiled.

Keesha turned and screamed as loud as she could. "SHUT UP!"

"Miss Mars?"

They turn to see Dean Van de Sant waiting at his office door.

"Please step inside my office."

"Why should I?" Lily didn't move.

"Because I asked you," the dean said, irritation registering in his voice.

"You're hardly in any position to boss people around."

Van de Sant knew this was only the beginning. Now that word of his affair with Olivia Abernathy was common knowledge, students would take the opportunity to challenge him, thinking he would shrink back out of embarrassment or shame. He had no intention of doing that. He was fairly sure he would lose his job over the issue, but he wasn't going to lose his self-respect before that happened.

Fuck you, you little whore, he thought as he smiled stiffly at the Mars girl. Then out loud, he said, "Your mother is waiting for you."

Lily's stomach tightened. She'd been so caught up in her grief over William she hadn't even thought about the repercussions of the affair. Glinda smirked but kept her creepy little mouth quiet. Keesha's face seemed to soften just a bit in sympathy. Lily glared at her classmates as she moved past the dean and entered his office.

Gwendolyn Mars sat primly behind the dean's desk, her blonde hair perfectly coiffed. She was wearing one of her favorite Chanel suits and looked like what she was—a debutante who had done everything right as she aged.

She stared at her daughter when she entered. The girl was a younger version of herself but with none of the inherent good sense that Gwendolyn had. When she'd gotten the call from one of her bridge partners, Celeste Taylor, about the drama that was unfolding at Danbury Prep, Gwendolyn couldn't believe what the woman was telling her. Her daughter had been having an affair with Bill Abernathy? Gwendolyn had even gone as far as to say, "What do you mean, an affair?" That just gave Celeste an opening to explain in graphic detail what people had been saying. "Your daughter has been having a sexual relationship with William Abernathy." Gwendolyn could hear the glee in her voice. Celeste delighted in watching other people make flaming messes of their lives.

Lily and William—it seemed absurd. Gwendolyn knew Bill. She didn't think he was the cheating type. He'd never so much as flirted with her, but he was screwing her daughter? Gwendolyn would never be able to live it down. These types of stories never died. Ten years from now, she and Lily could be out getting their nails done, and the other clients would whisper about it as they walked by like it just happened yesterday.

Lily stood silently. Gwendolyn knew she was waiting for her to speak. She had so much anger and embarrassment to convey, but decided to go with the truth. "I would have preferred you killed the man instead of sleep with him. At least then, you'd go away and I wouldn't have to deal with you."

32.SQUATTERS

Towering evergreens crowded both sides of the mountain road. Mason's dark gray Mustang eased along, turning in front of a sign that read, COZY PINE COTTAGES. The noise from the tires on the gravel parking lot shattered the quiet, disturbing a handful of crows who flew skyward.

"This is a lot of nature," Mason said as he and Kaylee approached the front door of the last building in the row. He looked out of place in his leather jacket and boots.

Kaylee reached around the door frame, feeling for something. "They used to keep a key up here." She moved a flower pot to look underneath. Still nothing.

Mason walked over to the front door and tried the handle.

"Of course they locked it. Otherwise they'd end up with squatters."

Mason took his time pulling out a pocket knife and opening it, fully enjoying the irony of the situation. "You mean people living here who don't belong? That would be terrible."

"Yes, it would be."

She watched as he used the knife to easily jimmy the flimsy lock. He held open the door for her to enter. "After you."

Inside, a large open space was neatly divided into a living area, dining area, and kitchen, with a door leading to what he assumed were the bedrooms. It was not quite as rustic as Mason expected, with tile countertops, curtains on the windows and warm wood floors. The furniture was covered with sheets. Mason yanked at one and sent up a cloud of dust.

"Do it slowly or we'll be sneezing the entire time we're here," Kaylee said. They moved to the sofa together and carefully folded the sheet off. "One summer when I was maybe nine years old, my family rented the house in front, the one nearest the road. An old couple used to live in this one. Anne and I spent a lot of time with them. We raked leaves, hung laundry. All sorts of things."

"So your fond childhood memories are of doing chores for people?"

They moved to another sheet, revealing a kitchen table.

"Yeah, actually. They made us feel helpful. And special. We also baked cookies and made pie and played card games with them. It was the best summer we ever had. Anne and I always said we'd come back someday. Maybe buy the place and live here forever."

"I thought you'd have gone to Europe or places like that for vacations."

"We did take trips to all sorts of amazing places. I'm not really sure how we ended up here that one summer. My mom and dad had been fighting a lot. I think he may have cut her off financially. Or maybe she just wanted to go somewhere he wouldn't want to follow. I don't know. Whatever the reason, Anne and I loved it."

"I can't picture your mom here."

"I don't remember much of her when we were here. I have no idea what she was doing when Anne and I were playing. It's not like she came out and climbed trees with us."

Mason smiled at the image. "Does the old couple still own it?"

"They were really old even then. They must have died. Their kids might still own it." She watched as he moved to the window and looked out. "These are all summer homes, so there's no one around to even see us." Kaylee moved behind him and put her arms around his waist, resting her head against his back. After a moment, she kissed his neck. He pulled away.

"It's totally private." She nibbled at his neck, but he pulled away again. "What?"

"Not right now."

"Why not?"

"Jesus, really? We left your father dead in a car trunk at your house."

"I know that."

"You think that's a turn-on?"

"Of course not."

"You think that makes me hot?"

"Why are you yelling at me? I said, 'of course not.'"

"I'm not yelling. I'm just reacting." Mason started going through the cabinets, eyeballing what little canned goods he saw. Most had labels with designs on them so old and outdated he knew they were expired. "I don't know how you can even think about anything like that right now."

"Why are you being so mean to me?"

"I'm not being mean. I'm just . . . I don't know what I am." He opened another cabinet and shook his head when he saw the contents. "Jesus. Look at all these teapots."

Kaylee thought for a moment before speaking. "I'm just . . . I don't know. I feel different. I'm free."

"Maybe not for long."

"I'm grateful. Okay?"

"So you're trying to thank me for what I did?"

"Gross. No. How could you say that?" She looked like he'd slapped her. "I know this is a bad situation. I'm freaked out about what happened. What's been happening the past few years."

Mason felt himself tense when she referenced the abuse. Why was he giving her crap knowing what she'd been through? He hated himself in that moment.

"The main thing I feel is relief," Kaylee continued. "Okay? I don't have anymore secrets from you."

"I get it. I'm sorry. I'm really sorry. I just need some time. You've been through a lot. We've both been through a lot. Let's just take it easy. Okay? Get settled in here first. We need to make sure we're safe."

"We're safe here."

Mason took her face in his hands. "I love you. Just give me a minute to adjust. To everything. Things happened, Kaylee. We don't have to talk about them, but we can't . . . I can't just pretend they didn't. I've never been fake with you and I'm not going to start now."

"This isn't over, is it?"

"The worst is."

He turned to open another cabinet before she could see the doubt etched on this face. If he'd looked at her, he would have seen the same.

33. FRESH AIR

Anne Abernathy looked around her bedroom. She'd managed to get rid of the Parisian-poster theme the designer had given it and replaced them with pictures of works from the modern artists she favored like Sterling Ruby. She also had an affinity for heart art. Any time she saw a photo, or statue, or anything of a heart, Anne bought it. She guessed that meant she had a romantic bent to her. Funny how her sister was the one who was got the real-life romance. Anne hadn't even dated yet. She'd been asked, of course, but no one interested her. They were all too eager. Her mother called her a late bloomer, like she was some sort of defective flower.

She neatly folded her favorite wool sweater and tucked it in her backpack, along with her toothbrush and the iPhone charging cable. She wasn't sure how long she'd be gone and she didn't want to be too obvious when she walked by the cops who were still lingering in the living room and kitchen.

She casually slung the pack on her back and headed out, stopping to speak to the uniformed police milling around the kitchen island. "I need to get some air."

One of the detectives gestured to the cop.

Anne walked calmly down the driveway and onto Maple Street, where Trevor's vintage burgundy Cadillac was parked. He sat at the wheel and was anxious when Anne got in.

"How are you, sweetie?"

"I'm fine."

"Really?"

"What do you think?" Anne's voice was tired. She looked at Trevor, worry on her face.

He nodded sympathetically and put the car in gear. "Kaylee hasn't responded to any of her texts."

"She doesn't want them to find her."

"Does she want you to?"

Anne was a bit insulted by the question. "Of course."

"Why do you think you can when they can't?"

"Because I know my sister."

"You're sure?"

"Just drive. I've got to get away from here."

"Where am I driving?"

"Get on the interstate north." She knew her sister well enough to know she'd go to the one place they had a sweetly innocent summer.

They cruised in silence for a bit, but Trevor couldn't take the quiet. He had a million questions for her. "There's a rumor going around school that they made you identify the body." Anne shakes her head. "They knew who it was because my mom called them and told them. Besides, I'm too young to do that."

"I figured, but that's what people are saying."

"People just want to have something to talk about."

"This definitely is something to talk about."

Anne nodded. "They're vultures."

"This must all be pretty shocking for you."

Anne stayed silent and looked straight ahead. Trevor waited for her to respond, but it was clear she wouldn't, so he tried to prompt her. "Losing your dad."

"It is."

"Did they ask about him and Kaylee?"

"Just drive, please." Anne adjusted the backpack at her feet. "I want to get to her before dark."

Mason pulled back the calico curtain and looked out the window, scanning for any signs of he didn't know what.

"No one followed us." Kaylee sat at the table, eating peanut butter from the jar with a spoon. She scraped the inside slowly, concentrating as if it were an important task.

"I'm afraid of the bears."

"Not a country boy, I take it."

"I can light a fire."

"Using a lighter doesn't count."

"You mean there's another way to light a fire?"

Kaylee smiled. Mason watched her, concern etched on his face. She used her finger along the rim of the peanut butter jar to get the last bit.

"You're hungry," Mason noted. Kaylee only nodded. Her mouth was too sticky to talk. "This place isn't safe. People will notice we're here."

"We'll be careful."

"We need to figure out where we'll go next."

"Can't we just rest for a little while?"

"We need to get as far away as possible."

"Eventually."

"Soon. But until then, I'm going to get some supplies."

Kaylee stood abruptly, ready to join him. He put his hand on her shoulder.

"You stay here. They're looking for a couple."

She sat back down. Mason kissed her forehead. "Any last requests?"

"Very funny."

Mason headed toward the door. Kaylee called out.

"Actually. I do. Have a last request. Nutter Butters."

"Done." He headed out the door. Kaylee moved to the window and watched as he drove off, the crunch of the Mustang's tires on the gravel parking lot so familiar and soothing. She remembered when she was here before, waiting for a sign she and Anne could go down to the Mallones' cottage. Mr. Mallone's old Chevy truck was incredibly loud. She and Anne would watch and listen for it. When he came back from the store, they'd run down, sure that he had some new project to do they could help with.

Kaylee looked around the cottage. She and Anne had spent many happy days here. She wondered what the Mallones would think of this mess she was in. Kaylee honestly didn't know. They were remarkably kind, but kept their opinions to themselves. In hindsight, they must have realized something was strange about two little rich girls being at Cozy Pines that summer. Maybe they noticed Olivia was hardly mothering material and took pity on them. Kaylee would never know.

She had no idea what Mrs. Mallone would think of the current situation, but she did know what she would do. She would make cookies and invite the girls to talk to her as they worked. It was such a simple thing, and Kaylee realized now, a great distraction from their troubles. It was easier to talk them through when they were busy doing something. Therapists should consider that approach. Baking therapy. She smiled at the thought. She would have to tell Anne next time she saw her. Anne. Kaylee wondered when she would see her sister next. The way Mason talked, they might be on the run forever. She couldn't bear that. At least now she knew Anne would never have to deal with their father.

Kaylee turned on the old transistor radio that sat on the wooden table next to the rocking chair. It crackled with static and she patiently moved the dial to tune it. "Police are looking for the daughter of a prominent Danbury businessman and her boyfriend in his bludgeoning death . . ." A man's voice urgently spoke. Static was making the rest hard to understand. ". . . Found body in trunk . . . William . . . of the year . . ." Kaylee snapped off the radio.

34. MAKE THE GUY WAIT

Trevor fiddled with the radio as he drove. It was getting harder to find good stations now that they were out of the city. The downside to his sweet Caddy was that it wasn't Bluetooth-enabled. He found some vintage U2 playing.

"This is going to have to do." Trevor apologized as he sat back. Anne gave a half smile. She wasn't going to engage him in conversation. *It's going to be a long drive*, Trevor thought. Or not. She wouldn't tell him where they were going, so he had no idea if it was a day trip or an overnighter. He was okay with either, but not knowing was hard. The landscape around them was monotonous. They passed tree after tree. Trevor was not what one would call a nature lover, and the smell of fresh pine generally made him think of bathrooms cleaned with Pine Sol.

He spotted a police cruiser tucked on the side of the road up ahead. "Oh crap. Cops." Anne looked over at the instrument panel. "Are you speeding?"

"No."

"Then don't worry about it. They're not looking for us."

Trevor still felt his heart racing as they passed the car. The officer behind the wheel didn't seem to look when they went by. He may have been reading something. Anne was right. "I don't think I have the fortitude to be a fugitive," Trevor said. He looked over to Anne for a response, but she was lost in thought, her mind playing over the events of the last twenty-four hours.

The night before had started out so ordinary. Kaylee was getting ready for Keesha's party. As usual, she tried on almost every dress in her closet. Anne sat on her bed and talked to her as the moved about the room. "It's Keesha's house, so do you think that means I should dress more girlie? Or dress normal and wear white gloves?"

"Don't dress more girlie, but remember to always stick your pinky out when you drink." Anne demonstrated by holding a pretend teacup with her little finger extended.

"More like this." Kaylee threw back her head fast, doing a quick pretend shot, with her pinky extended. "Classy, right?" Anne laughed.

Kaylee pulled out another dress, a gray jersey with leather trim on the shoulders. "Why is this so hard?"

"I don't know. You look good in everything."

"You always say that. You sound like a mother."

"What mother are you talking about who always says you look nice?"

"One I saw in a movie once." They laughed, both knowing support wasn't exactly their mother's strong suit, but she did have good taste and passed it along to her daughters.

Kaylee pulled a creamy dress flecked with little black birds on it over her head.

Anne eyeballed her. "You could go to church in that."

Kaylee went to the closet that was off her bathroom and slipped on a short brown leather jacket before modeling it.

"Much better."

"Okay. Now. Shoes." Anne fell backward onto the bed in mock exhaustion.

"Isn't Mason supposed to be here soon?"

"He was supposed to be here ten minutes ago, but apparently he's late."

"I thought the girl was supposed to make the guy wait. Not the other way around."

"You've been listening to Mom too much."

"Are you guys okay?"

"Yeah. We're good. I don't think this is anything."

"Okay." Anne was skeptical. "It's just really unusual for him."

"Maybe there was traffic or he had trouble with his car."

"Wouldn't he call you?"

"Maybe his battery is dead. Are you trying to make me worry?"

"No. Of course not. It's just weird."

Kaylee pulled out her phone and hit a button. "You're making me worry."

"Sorry."

Kaylee listened as the phone rang. When voice mail kicked in, she hung up, giving her sister an exaggerated glare.

"It's probably nothing."Anne was contrite. She didn't want to stress her sister out. But she really was wondering where Mason was.

Kaylee pulled on some boots and then pulled them off. She tried several black heels before settling on a pair of basic pumps. Anne wasn't a fan of the choice. "Your feet are going to hurt."

"I'm not hiking in them. I'll just be standing around for a few hours." She checked her phone.

"Still no word?"

Kaylee shot her sister a dirty look, and then dialed her phone and waited as it rang. "Hey. It's me. Wondering where you are. I'm starting to get worried. And Anne is really, really worried." She stuck her tongue out at her. "When you get this, text me. Or call me. Or, better yet, come get me. Otherwise I'm going to hitch to Keesha's. That's what they call it, right? The thing with the thumb?"

As soon as she hung up, her phone rang and she quickly answered with a smile. "Where are you?"

"Oh. Hi." She shook her head as she listened to the person talking. "I'm waiting for Mason." She paused. "You heard he's there already? That's weird. Then can you come and pick me up?" She paused. "Okay. See you soon."

She hung up.

"Abby from cheerleading heard Mason's already at Keesha's."

"Are you sure he was supposed to come get you?"

"Um. Yes." Kaylee said in a "duh" tone.

"So Abby was calling you to get some gossip?"

"Again. Yes." Duh. "She seems to know more than I do and is on her way to get me." Kaylee looked at the pile of clothes at the foot of her bed. "What a mess."

"I'll clean this up later. Go finish your makeup." Anne nodded toward the bathroom. "When you find out what's going on with Mason, text me."

35. OTHERWISE, WHAT'S THE POINT?

Mason drove along the mountain road. To one side, the tree-covered hill rose straight from the road. To the other, the hill continued downward. Nestled on that downward slope was a service station, its roof almost even with the road. Mason eased the Mustang on the steep driveway and pulled in front. The place was like something out of the 1950s, with an old ice machine against the barn-type doors to the garage and a hand-painted sign that said, MECHANIC. Another nearby advertised: NIGHT CRAWLERS. He entered the door to the right of it. Inside was the mom-and-pop equivalent of a minimart. Refrigerators lined one wall. A coffee station was tucked in one corner. Mason went over and poured a cup and something resembling black tar came out. He paused, sniffed it, then took a tentative sip. It tasted worse than it looked. He pitched it in the trash and went looking for supplies. Almost immediately he found the Nutter Butters. Score! Kaylee would be pleased and that made him smile.

He grabbed some Cokes, some waters, and a few other staples—ground coffee, milk, bread, and some deli meats. She would be begging for a salad in no time. He wasn't sure how long they would be in this part of the state. They weren't that far from the Canadian border, but they didn't have passports and he wasn't sure what they needed to cross over. Mason thought it was probably safest to stay put a few more days until police wouldn't be quite so interested in finding them.

He still couldn't believe what had happened after Keesha's party. He promised Kaylee they wouldn't talk about it, but he couldn't help thinking about it. She was much more traumatized, obviously, than he was. He wondered what exactly happened last night that was different than any other night with her father. What made her bludgeon him then, and not yesterday or last week? He hoped his breaking up with her was not what pushed her over the edge, but he suspected it was at least part of the reason. He wouldn't have thought her capable of what he saw in the garage, the kind of rage it must have taken to do that kind of damage to a person. But there was a lot he didn't know about her, that was so clear now. He felt tremendously guilty for not picking up something was wrong. All the signs were there. He wished he'd been smart enough to see them. He would never let her down like that again, he told himself.

He took his items to the counter and paid quickly with cash. The old woman behind the register barely made eye contact with him.

Once outside, Mason tensed. A young, curly-haired, blond guy in greasy coveralls was looking inside the window of the Mustang. "Can I help you with something?" Mason knew the police had probably alerted the news outlets with a description of his car. But the mechanic didn't seem uncomfortable when he approached him. "Nice ride." He smiled openly.

Mason felt himself relax a little. "Thanks."

"V8?"

Mason nodded. "Otherwise, what's the point?" He started putting the groceries in the trunk, keeping an eye on the guy as he admired the car from various angles.

"How fast does she go?"

"How fast does she go, or how fast have I gone? Supposedly she'll top out at one hundred ninety."

"How high have you taken her?"

"One hundred."

"You got more control than me."

"I've got a big fear of losing my license and an even bigger one of what my father would do if I got caught doing anything near one hundred ten. Or one hundred twenty."

"But still."

"Still."

"I rode in a Corvette once that went up to one hundred twenty."

"Sick."

"Like being in a rocket."

Mason looked up past his new friend toward the road. His face darkened. He saw Trevor's very distinct burgundy Cadillac drive by. Shit! How did he know where to find them? Then a dark SUV with two men in in the front seat passed, traveling behind Trevor at a discreet distance. Mason knew instinctively they were cops.

He looked at the mechanic, and then back up at the road. He had to warn Kaylee. He wished he hadn't thrown out their phones.

36.THE CHASE

"How much do you think that thing is worth?" Detective Miguel Acosta asked his partner, Harry Duke, as they followed the '62 Cadillac.

"How the hell should I know? Google it." Duke thought they were wasting time following the murder suspect's sister.

"When I was his age, I took my girlfriends on dates on my bicycle."

"Like you had dates in high school."

Kaylee licked some peanut butter off her thumb and then moved to the kitchen sink to wash her hands. She turned on the faucet and brown water spurted out, drenching her. She jumped back, lamenting the splash marks on her dress. It was the same dress she picked so carefully the night before to go to Keesha's party. She felt like she'd aged twenty years in the last day. She had no idea what came next. Mason seemed to have a decent amount of cash, but she didn't ask where he got it. Everything was happening so quickly, she wasn't sure she wanted to know. She was certain of one thing: she would stand by Mason no matter what. He'd done something she'd wanted to do for at least two years. He killed her father.

Anne and Trevor drove past the COZY PINE COTTAGES sign and pulled off the road onto the gravel shoulder where it widened a bit. He parked close to the trees and they got out.

"This is such a conspicuous car." Anne stared at the prominent fins.

"What can I say? Subtle is not my thing." Trevor used his cardigan sleeve to buff a smudge off the car door. Anne grabbed some dry brush and dragged it behind the car, trying to camouflage it. Trevor watched. "Please don't scratch my paint unless you really think this is going to work."

Anne dropped the branch she was holding. "Let's go find Kaylee."

She walked up the road toward the cabins. Trevor followed.

"I did not dress for something so rustic." He was still in his Danbury uniform. "I would totally not fit in at a square dance."

"You would not fit in at a square anything."

"True that."

Anne started feeling around the familiar door frame for a key. She immediately found one, put it in the lock, and jiggled until it slid open. She was turning the knob when a man's voice commanded, "Don't move."

Anne froze. Trevor immediately put his hands over his head. He felt faintly ridiculous, but he wasn't about to get shot. He looked over his shoulder. There was a tall African American policeman who looked like he could break Trevor in two, and his partner, a shorter Latino who also looked like he could do some serious damage. Trevor realized a lot of people in law enforcement probably could snap him like a twig.

Anne still faced the door, contemplating her next move.

"Step away from the door." Acosta ordered with a steady voice.

Anne nodded slowly. Then in a voice so surprisingly loud, even Trevor jumped, she yelled, "Kaylee! If you're in there, run!"

"Christ." Duke pushed her aside and Acosta opened the door. Guns drawn, they entered the house. The furniture was covered with sheets. Acosta gestured and they entered, military style, one taking point and visually clearing the area before the other followed. Anne and Trevor waited outside.

The two cops ran out the front door, glaring at Anne as they passed. Acosta barked at them. "Don't even think about going anywhere."

Trevor and Anne watched as Duke and Acosta stood in the courtyard, eyeballing each of the little buildings. "They've got to be here somewhere," Acosta said. Finally, Duke spotted a curtain moving in the last cottage in the row. "There!" They moved toward it.

Trevor felt a desperate urge to help Kaylee. He stepped in front of the cops. "Officers, if you just stop for a minute . . ."

"MOVE!" The Latino cop pointed his gun at Trevor, who put up his hands and backed away.

"Since you put it that way." He got the hell out of the way and let the cops run past.

A patrolman sat in his car tucked out of sight of Route 1, the state road that ran north and south along the whole eastern part of the country. This particular stretch was straight and fun to drive fast because it had a slight rolling quality. If you hit the uphills just right, you caught a little air on the downslope.

At the moment, he was doing a crossword puzzle from the back of one of his wife's celebrity magazines, trying to figure out which actor appeared in both the shows *The Neighbors* and *The Secret Life of the American Teenager*. He glanced up as a sweet Mustang drove past. It was going fast, but not fast enough to bother stopping it.

His radio crackled to life. "We have an APB out for Danbury murder suspects. Male, eighteen, six feet tall. Brown hair.

Female, seventeen. Long brown hair. Suspects last seen driving newer model dark gray Mustang with temporary plates."

The cop put his pen down. He looked out the window of his car. A dark gray Mustang had just driven past. He turned on his engine and did a U-turn out of his hiding spot. He sped forward and quickly saw the Mustang in the distance, with only one person inside. "Possible sighting of suspect vehicle on Highway One northbound below the Route Five junction. In pursuit," he said quickly into the radio. With a flip of the switch, his lights strobed and siren wailed.

He floored it, accelerating and expecting a full-on chase. But he nearly rammed into the back of the Mustang. The driver wasn't trying to get away. The Mustang's right-side turn signal blinked on, preparing to pull over. The patrol officer tailed the car as it slowly drifted to the shoulder.

"Approaching one suspect in vehicle. Appears to be male." He hung the handset back on the cradle before the dispatcher spoke back. "Be careful, Lou. Remember suspects are wanted for murder."

Lou was aware. He approached the Mustang with his gun drawn. This kid was a killer, and Lou wanted to go home to his family that night.

Duke and Acosta entered the cottage, guns drawn. Signs of life were everywhere. The sheets had been removed from most of the furniture. An empty peanut-butter container sat on the kitchen table. They quickly eyeballed their surroundings.

"Shit. Back door," Acosta said as he entered the mudroom and saw the rear entrance. "It's open." Whoever was there had fled out the back. He and Duke rushed to follow.

When they were gone, the sheet covering one of the taller bar-height tables in the corner of the living room slowly moved. Kaylee crawled out from underneath. She crept silently, like a cat and headed toward the front door of the cabin. She looked over her shoulder before slowly opening it. A figure blocked her. She screamed, and he covered her mouth.

The patrol officer went up to the driver's side of the Mustang. A young man of about seventeen smiled warmly at him. "I don't think I was speeding, officer."

"You need to put your hands on the steering wheel where I can see them."

"Sure." He obeyed and the cop took a closer look through the open window.

"Billy, is that you?" The kid mechanic from the service station up the road smiled back at him. "What the hell are you doing with this car?"

"Some guy at the station gave it to me. Alls I had to do was drop him down by those cottages."

"Shit."

———

Mason held his hand over Kaylee's mouth. He put a finger to his lips, gesturing for her to be quiet. She relaxed and hugged him. "Police are here," she whispered. He nodded and took her by the hand, walking out the front of the cabin. Anne and Trevor were still standing where the cops had commanded them to stay. Kaylee felt herself grin when she saw her little sister. She pulled toward her, ready to hug, but Anne shook her head and mouthed the word, *Go!*

Once they were clear of the steps, Mason and Kaylee ran full throttle toward the road. They crossed the parking lot and were heading around the manager's cabin when the sound of a gun cocking stopped them. "Freeze."

They turned to face an African American man in a tie, pointing a gun at them. Mason looked back over his own shoulder and saw another plainclothes cop was behind them. They were surrounded. Kaylee clutched his arm.

"Step away from the girl," Acosta said. But Kaylee was holding Mason tight. "Step away!"

Mason turned and pried Kaylee's fingers from his arm as he spoke to the cops. "You really don't have to worry about her. It's me you want." He dropped down to his knees.

Kaylee tried to pull him up. "Mason, no!" Duke put a firm hand on her shoulder and pulled her away from him.

"I killed her father."

"No! Don't say anything. Don't do this!" Kaylee was nearing hysteria. She couldn't believe what was happening.

Mason put his hands on the back of his head and waited for the cops to grab him. They pushed him to the ground and pulled his hands behind his back. He addressed Kaylee as they cuffed him, urgency in his voice. "I did it Kaylee. Me. I'm sorry, but it was all me." He eyeballed her, willing her to understand his message. He knew she did it, but he helped hide the body. And there was no use in both of them going to prison. He knew he could survive anywhere as much as he knew she couldn't. His choice to take the fall for her crime was the only one that made sense.

The notebook page was filled with quickly scribbled cursive. Mason sat at the table in the police interrogation room and reread what he'd written. Satisfied, he signed his name at the bottom and then spoke at the two-way mirror across from him. "There. You have what you need."

Duke came in and picked up the notebook. He took his time reading the page before putting it back on the table. "You didn't say what the murder weapon was."

"How about I confess the way I want?"

"We would be more convinced about everything if you could tell us what the murder weapon was."

"If you don't want my confession, just say so." Mason held out his hand like he expected the detective to give it back. He was trying hard to play it tough, but inside, he felt sick. He had no idea what the murder weapon was, or where it was. Kaylee had asked not to talk about what happened, and he'd honored her request.

"You want to go to trial, it's up to you." Duke left the room and joined his partner on the other side of the two-way mirror. A uniformed police officer walked by them, escorting Kaylee. "Send her in," Acosta told him. The two detectives watched as she flew toward Mason and hugged him. "Are you okay? Did they hurt you?"

"Why are we doing this?" the uniformed officer asked the detectives.

"We want to see if it was a joint effort."

Inside the room, Kaylee whispered to Mason. "I think they're watching us." Mason nodded. Of course they were watching. And listening. He took the chair he'd been sitting on and picked it up. The detectives on the other side of the mirror took notice, but Duke gestured for them to stand down. That changed the second he realized Mason was using the chair to prop under the doorknob into the room, effectively locking everyone out. Several cops converged on it, trying to push the door open. Duke and Acosta stayed put, watching them. Mason spoke quickly. He realized they didn't have much time.

"Kaylee, I want to talk to you, but I need it to be private. . . ." As he spoke, he traced a wire that ran along the wall. "A lot has gone on in the past twenty-four hours, and what we do next will influence the rest of our lives."

He traced the line to where it disappeared into the wall. Duke knew what was coming next. "Smart little son of a bitch."

"So you listen . . ." The detective watched as Mason yanked the cord out of the wall. He continued speaking to Kaylee, but all the detective heard was the static of the broken wire.

Mason dropped the wire and held Kaylee by the shoulders. "No matter what you do, don't tell them what you did."

"What do you mean? What I did?" Behind them, cops pounded on the blocked door.

"To your father. Don't tell them what you did to your father."

"I didn't do anything to him."

"Kaylee, we don't have time for these games. I found him on the floor. I know you killed him."

"I didn't do that. I wish I did, but I didn't. I swear."

"He was already dead when I got to your house, Kaylee."

"That's impossible." She shook her head. They both were reaching the same terrible conclusion.

"If you didn't kill him. And I didn't, then who did?"

Behind them, the cops finally broke the door open and flooded the room. They grabbed Mason and slammed him into a wall, swatting away Kaylee when she tried to stop them. Another cop pinned her arms behind her back. She watched as Acosta entered and scooped up the notebook with Mason's signed confession from the table.

They dragged Mason out the door. "Kaylee. Just don't say anything. Nothing. We'll figure this out."

"I love you, Mason."

"I love you too. Don't forget that."

EPILOGUE

Trevor drove as Anne sat quietly next to him. Her brow was furrowed. Trevor was practically bursting with the need to go over what had just happened. Surely, she didn't expect to ride the entire way back to Danbury in silence.

"So it was Mason. I still can't believe it. I mean, I know he has a temper and he can be violent, but I still hoped it wasn't true." Trevor wanted Kaylee to have some happiness. That seemed unlikely now.

"I don't think he did it." Anne was resolute.

"I don't want to believe it either, but he confessed."

"Still."

Something about her voice seemed odd. Trevor glanced at her and then returned his focus to the road. "I mean, you don't confess to murder for no reason."

"Just drive, please."

Anne was thinking of the previous night. Kaylee had gotten dressed for the party and then hurried off when she heard Mason was already there. Anne was worried he'd been mad about something. She loved that her sister had someone like Mason in her life.

Anne had told her sister she'd clean the clothes hurricane she'd left behind. As soon as Kaylee was gone, she started picking up dresses and hanging them and lining discarded heels on shelves in the closet. It was when she was doing that that she saw the award tucked way in the back of the row of shoes Anne knew Kaylee hardly ever wore. She pulled it out and felt its heavy weight. Kaylee had stolen their father's award from the Danbury Prep trophy case. Anne knew exactly why. She'd sat in the audience and watched him give his acceptance speech and felt sick as the audience laughed at his charming comments. Kaylee could only have felt worse.

"What are you doing with that?" A voice startled her. She turned and faced the man himself. He must have gotten home from work and was searching for Kaylee. Anne knew why. She stared at him. He was a monster.

"I asked you where that came from?"

The rest wasn't exactly clear in her head. She knew he'd tried to pull it from her, and somehow she'd managed to get out of the bedroom. He chased her. She wasn't sure if he wanted the award or something else.

The next thing she knew, she was at school and the guidance counselor was telling her someone had died. Anne remembered how strange it was to stand outside the school and not hear anything. But when she thought it was quiet, a faint buzzing sound began. It grew louder. Until finally, she could make out some words. "Are you okay?"

Trevor had watched her zone out and was worried. "Are you okay? Do you feel faint?"

Anne smiled at him and shifted in the car seat. "I'm fine. Sorry. It's just been stressful."

Trevor nodded and focused on the road.

She adjusted the backpack at her feet. The top zipper wasn't shut properly and her favorite sweater was pushing out, as well as the tip of her father's crystal community award. Flecks of dried blood dotted its shiny surface.

Philadelphia native BETH SZYMKOWSKI
wrote her first piece of fiction when she was in the
second grade. It involved a treehouse and a sur-
gery gone horribly wrong. She's been writing ever
since. Beth attended Duke University and started
her professional career as a journalist in North
Carolina, where she developed a deep appreciation for communicating volumes while saying
little. She's written screenplays for Disney, ABC
Family, and many others, including the original
screenplay for the Runaways series. Beth lives in
Los Angeles with a dog, a tarantula, and the occasional praying mantis, along with her two sons.

You can follow her on
Twitter @longtallbeth

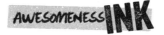

1// WHITNEY

Buzz. Buzz. Buzz.

"Hello?"

"Hey, Little Orphan Whitney!" The girl's voice sounds friendly but I know it's anything but. "Put down those pills, pusher! The sun will come out tomorrow. *Not.*" I hear uproarious laughter and then a dial tone.

Outside my room, footsteps sound like a herd of elephants.

"Sam, get over here! You've got to get to bed!"

"Try and make me! I'm not tired and I'm not going to bed."

"Enough games, Sam. You're thirteen. I'm twenty-three, which means I'm in charge and I don't care if you're tired. You have school tomorrow. You have to get to sleep." Keith sounds exasperated—like he always does by this time of night.

"Sucks to be you. You'll have to catch me if you want me in my room."

They run by my door so fast, the ribbons I've won in band competitions sway on my mirror. I hear their voices echo, even though they're all the way down the hall. Our house has six bedrooms and a long, hardwood-floor hallway overlooking the downstairs. I remember a time when my brothers raced across it in their roller hockey skates. They're making so much noise tonight, I suspect Sam and Keith are in their bare feet.

Buzz. Buzz. Buzz.

My cell phone vibrates again as the shouting in the hall intensifies. I'm afraid to know who's calling me. The screen says: NO CALLER ID and when that happens, it's never a good thing.

Don't answer it. It's just the She-Bitches again, I think. *Be strong.*

But I pick up.

I try to sound upbeat. "Hello?"

"Aww, she must really need a friend." I hear one of the She-Bitches say. "She picked up on the first ring. Loser." *Click.*

The She-Bitches, as I call our school's Queen Bee and her relentless minions, hate my best friend, Susan, and me. I suspect it has something to do with the fact we're what you'd call band geeks. I guess Melanie can't handle that her new boyfriend, Scott Dwyer, used to like a dork like me.

BOOM!

I hear something slam into the wall outside my room and jump. I'd recognize Zak's crazy laugh anywhere. He's been my brother's best friend since the fifth grade, even though Zak's a year older. "Dude, I said catch!"

"You freak! Who throws balls in the house?" My older brother

Jason, who's a junior, is a baseball god at our school. At least he used to be before things started falling apart.

"You're not throwing balls anywhere or catching them either." I hear Zak reply. "Try going to practice once in a while. Here! Try another one!"

I hear glass shatter and wince.

"What are you guys doing? Dad bought Mom that vase in Mexico!" I hear Keith shout. My heart sinks. I know what vase he's talking about. Mom used to collect abstract crystal vases and that pink one, shaped like a flamingo's neck, was one of her favorites. "I know I'm not Dad, but you can't keep . . ."

My phone buzzes again and I close my eyes. "Please make them stop," I whisper to myself. "Please make them all stop."

"What the hell was that?" My sister, Lexi, snaps. "I was in the middle of shaving my legs when I heard a crash and freakin' cut myself."

Buzz. Buzz. Buzz.

"Sorry we interrupted you slutting yourself up," Jason retorts. I hear a smack. "OEUF! That hurt!" As his twin, Lexi can get away with shelling out a little abuse now and then.

"If Lexi's going out, I'm going out—or at least not going to bed," Sam tries again. The youngest of my siblings is anything but the quiet one.

That would be me.

Buzz. Buzz. Buzz. They're ringing again. I might as well get this over with.

"Hello?"

"Pathetic answering for a third time, Whitney!" A new She-Bitch is on the line. "Why don't you do us all a favor and disappear like your daddy?" A group of girls bursts out laughing and hang up.

"You're not staying up, Sam!"

"What do you mean, 'slutting myself up'? How dare you say that!"

On the other side of this door, just inches from where I sit on my bed, surrounded by twinkle lights I've had strung up since Christmas, another Connolly storm is brewing. It's pretty much the same storm we've had every night since Dad left. I take that back—*before* Dad left, when Mom died. Dirty laundry is piled high in the hallways, the kitchen sink is overflowing with dirty dishes, there's crap crammed in every corner of this big, once well-taken-care-of house where Keith lives again, forced to leave medical school to take care of us. The whole situation sucks way more than I ever imagined.

As my phone starts to buzz again, I get up from my bed and walk toward the hand-painted white dresser I've had since I was five. Ditto the dollhouse Mom lovingly decorated for me that still sits on it. I can't part with it, just like I can't part with this family, however warped it's become.

I open my top drawer and take out the orange bottle with the white security cap and smile just a little when I read the medication's warning label. SIDE EFFECTS: MAY CAUSE MUSICAL HALLUCINATIONS. I open the bottle and pop one blue-and-white capsule into my mouth and swallow. I close my eyes and wait.

When I open my eyes again, the world is as it should be, shrouded in a rainbow of colors that make everything just a little bit brighter and cheerier like that scene in *Mary Poppins* when Bert and Mary jump through the painting. (Mom and I watched that movie at least fifteen times together. Probably fifteen more when she was going through chemo.) The best part of the hallucinations, though, is the singing. No more shouting. No more name-calling. Life becomes my own personal music video.

"I walk these halls as the lights go out," I sing. "Each night the same. I think I'm going insane."

I stare into the floor-length mirror in my room and a more confident me stares back. Gone are the jeans I've had for two years and the faded blue sweatshirt that has seen better days. My new ensemble is straight from *Vogue*. My long, curly hair looks shiny rather than unruly and my eyes and olive skin that I got courtesy of my South Pacific/Asian mother and Caucasian dad suddenly seem exotic. The "new" me isn't just a band geek. I can actually sing, as can the rest of my family and friends.

"We're falling apart, can't bear to be real, something inside us filled with such fear," I sing. "It would hurt too much to admit he left. What's wrong with us? Why can't we forget? Sweet little pill, take me away. Make me hallucinate, I just can't stay." The sounds in the hall fade away, and it's just me in my own happy world.

I fought Keith when he took me to the doctor. The last thing I wanted was to be on "meds." I thought medication meant I needed a straitjacket or the loony bin, but my psychiatrist, Dr. Martin, said the pills would help me cope with a mom who had been sick for too long and a dad who up and left us in the middle of the night. Paxil made me loopy. Cymbalta made me want to Hulk out. But this new one, which seems to turn my most stressful moments into musical numbers, I can handle. That's why I haven't told anyone about the side effects. Who doesn't want life to feel like an episode of *Glee*?

"Sweet little pill, take me away," the me in the mirror sings. "Falling apart at the end of the day."

I open the door just a crack and instead of fighting, my brothers, sister, and Zak are singing too. This house, which used to look like it belonged in a Pottery Barn catalog, is exactly that way again. The laundry has disappeared. Couch cushions aren't stained or missing. Mom's vase isn't broken; late bills and final notices aren't lying on an antique hall table. Maybe if I sing hard enough, Dad will be back downstairs in our chef's kitchen, flipping homemade pancakes.

Buzz. Buzz. Buzz.

When my phone vibrates again, a dose of reality takes over. When I see the caller ID, I pick up immediately. I throw myself back on my bed and hug the turquoise pillow that doubles as my teddy bear. "Hey!"

"Did the She-Bitches call you too?" Susan sounds as tightly wound as I felt a few minutes ago. Melanie's crew are banshees dressed in J.Crew. It's not a pretty combo. "Tonight they seemed obsessed with my boobs—or lack thereof."

I sigh. "They called me a pill popper and wished I'd vanish like my dad." I twirl a loose thread from my turquoise-and-white zebra print comforter around my pinkie finger and stare at the lights strung along my ceiling. "Tell me again why people call high school the best time of our lives? Ninth grade blows."

"I couldn't agree more," she says. Then she's silent for a moment. "Whit? Promise me you won't call your dad again. Calling him will only make you feel worse."

"I know," I say. But I don't really mean it.

"He's been gone for six months and hasn't tried to reach you guys once," Susan reminds me. "Leaving yet another message is going to make you go postal."

I wince. Susan means well, but the Dad topic is still a thorny one.

"Sam?" Keith's voice travels from the other end of the hallway, probably near my parents' master suite that's closed up like a tomb. "Wherever you are, get to bed. Now!"

"Fine," Sam says wearily, finally tired of fighting. "I'll go. Night."

"Jason, privacy please?"

"From what I've heard, Lexi, you're anything but the private type," Jason says. Lexi hits him again.

"Geez, is that any way to talk to your sister?" Zak asks.

"Shut up, Zak!" they say in unison as the twins sometimes do. Zak is always here these days. He's like an unofficial sixth sibling, which is an odd thing to say when I think of how much he flirts with Lexi.

Several doors slam and then the house is as quiet as I've heard it all night. My body relaxes.

"I can't help myself," I say. "If he doesn't come back soon, we're toast. Just like my self-esteem."

"Pick it up off the floor and get some sleep," Susan commands. "I'll see you in the morning for band."

I hang up and stare at the phone in my hand contemplating what to do. *Call again. Don't call.* I feel like I have both an angel and devil on my shoulder. I turn to my side and stare at the picture of my parents on their wedding day. My mother's hair is windswept, and the lei she's wearing is blowing in the Honolulu breeze. They got married on the beach, just the two of them. Maybe that's why they look so happy. "You look just like your mom," I can hear Dad tell me. He said that the night I found him in the garden looking at a box of pictures from all our vacations, sports games . . . basically any and all of our happier moments. Mom always said she was going to put those pictures in albums, but in the end she never had a chance. "I miss those days," I remember him saying as he stared at a picture of all of us at Emmet State Park where we went camping every summer. "I'd give anything to get them back."

I hit REDIAL on my phone and listen to it ring. As suspected the voice mail picks up. "Hi, you've reached David Connolly. Please leave a message."

"Dad, this is like the hundredth message I've left you," I say, hating how desperate I sound. "Where are you? You have to come back. Keith had to leave med school, Jason hasn't hit a baseball all season, Sam is being, well, Sam, and Lexi is going for a new title—Bimbo of the Year. You said that night that you were just . . . well, you know what you said. Just get back here. Please."

BEEP! "This voice mailbox is full," a computerized voice tells me.

I throw my phone down in disgust. Through the vent in my room, I can hear Keith talking to someone that's definitely not my sister. The next sounds are ones I definitely want to block from my mind. I close my eyes and every color of the rainbow stares back at me.

That's when I hear my window fly open. I open my eyes and see a guy in a ripped tee, guyliner, and various skull tattoos climbing inside. I let out an ear-piercing scream and grab my nightstand lamp as a weapon. Then I realize it's just Lexi's loser boyfriend, Jared.

He holds his hands up to surrender, which, knowing him, he's probably had to do several times with the cops. "Whitney, chill! Wrong window."

"*Get out of here,*" I whisper loudly.

He climbs back over the ledge just as Keith busts through my door. "What happened?" he says, sounding out of breath. I notice his shirt is half-unbuttoned. "Why'd you scream?" My oldest brother, dark-haired with rings under his eyes to match, looks tired, but not *too* tired.

"Nightmare," I lie, and Keith gives me a look. I wonder why I'm covering for the new Lexi again. I guess I don't think Keith can handle any more than he already is. "Night terrors actually. Medication side effects," I add since he doesn't seem to be buying my story. "Who's that?" I motion to the petite blonde with the pin-straight hair hovering behind him.

Keith's cheeks color. "No one. Go to sleep. I'll see you in the morning."

He shuts my door behind him. I wait till I hear him and his blonde walk down the hall and shut Keith's door before I venture out of my room. I creak down the long hallway of our home, which was once the envy of all the moms in my elementary school car pool. ("Oh, Dianne, you're so lucky your husband is in real estate and could find a steal like this in Southern California!") My dad said when he convinced my mom to buy this house right after the twins were born, it was a money pit that had to be gutted from top to bottom. Over time, this place went from a dump to the jewel of our suburban street.

I head straight to Lexi's room, which looks like a tornado destroyed a fashion warehouse. Clothes are all over the floor, her bed is a crumpled mess, papers litter her dresser and desk. The room is empty, so I try the bathroom she shares with Jason. When I hover near the door—spying, my siblings would call it—I see her getting ready to go out. She's probably meeting up with that loser Jared again. What is she thinking? Instead of stressing out, I let the side effects take over and see a comforting hallucination: Lexi rocking out to her favorite Kesha song, "C'Mon." The only thing that would make this moment better is if my moody sister let me dance around the room with her and join her in song.

Wait a minute. This is my side effect. Within seconds, Lexi and I are both in her room, lost in the music, and singing together about how fun it would be to go out tonight and not have another care in the world.

And for a moment, I'd give anything for the hallucination to come true.